No Disguise for Love

Narda looked up at the Marquis.

"Thank you," she said in a soft voice, "for bringing me with you."

"I can only hope your journey is rewarded by your finding what you seek," the Marquis said.

She looked so lovely that the Marquis suddenly had an almost uncontrollable desire to kiss her.

He had only to stretch out his arms and pull her close to him.

The Marquis turned away.

"Good-night, Narda," he said, "and sleep well. . . ."

*A Camfield Novel of Love
by Barbara Cartland*

"Barbara Cartland's novels are all distinguished by their intelligence, good sense, and good nature. . . ."
—ROMANTIC TIMES

"Who could give better advice on how to keep your romance going strong than the world's most famous romance novelist, Barbara Cartland?"
—THE STAR

Camfield Place,
Hatfield
Hertfordshire,
England

Dearest Reader,

Camfield Novels of Love mark a very exciting era of my books with Jove. They have already published nearly two hundred of my titles since they became my first publisher in America, and now all my original paperback romances in the future will be published exclusively by them.

As you already know, Camfield Place in Hertfordshire is my home, which originally existed in 1275, but was rebuilt in 1867 by the grandfather of Beatrix Potter.

It was here in the lovely house, with the best view in the county, that she wrote *The Tale of Peter Rabbit*. Mr. McGregor's garden is exactly as she described it. The door in the wall that the fat little rabbit could not squeeze underneath and the goldfish pool where the white cat sat twitching its tail are still there.

I had Camfield Place blessed when I came here in 1950 and was so happy with my husband until he died, and now with my children and grandchildren, that I know the atmosphere is filled with love and we have all been very lucky.

It is easy here to write of love and I know you will enjoy the Camfield Novels of Love. Their plots are definitely exciting and the covers very romantic. They come to you, like all my books, with love.

Bless you,

CAMFIELD NOVELS OF LOVE
by Barbara Cartland

THE POOR GOVERNESS
WINGED VICTORY
LUCKY IN LOVE
LOVE AND THE MARQUIS
A MIRACLE IN MUSIC
LIGHT OF THE GODS
BRIDE TO A BRIGAND
LOVE COMES WEST
A WITCH'S SPELL
SECRETS
THE STORMS OF LOVE
MOONLIGHT ON THE
   SPHINX
WHITE LILAC
REVENGE OF THE HEART
THE ISLAND OF LOVE
THERESA AND A TIGER
LOVE IS HEAVEN
MIRACLE FOR A
   MADONNA
A VERY UNUSUAL WIFE
THE PERIL AND
   THE PRINCE
ALONE AND AFRAID
TEMPTATION OF A
   TEACHER
ROYAL PUNISHMENT
THE DEVILISH
   DECEPTION
PARADISE FOUND
LOVE IS A GAMBLE
A VICTORY FOR LOVE
LOOK WITH LOVE
NEVER FORGET LOVE

HELGA IN HIDING
SAFE AT LAST
HAUNTED
CROWNED WITH LOVE
ESCAPE
THE DEVIL DEFEATED
THE SECRET OF
   THE MOSQUE
A DREAM IN SPAIN
THE LOVE TRAP
LISTEN TO LOVE
THE GOLDEN CAGE
LOVE CASTS OUT FEAR
A WORLD OF LOVE
DANCING ON A RAINBOW
LOVE JOINS THE CLANS
AN ANGEL RUNS AWAY
FORCED TO MARRY
BEWILDERED IN BERLIN
WANTED—A WEDDING
   RING
THE EARL ESCAPES
STARLIGHT OVER TUNIS
THE LOVE PUZZLE
LOVE AND KISSES
SAPPHIRES IN SIAM
A CARETAKER OF LOVE
SECRETS OF THE HEART
RIDING IN THE SKY
LOVERS IN LISBON
LOVE IS INVINCIBLE
THE GODDESS OF LOVE
AN ADVENTURE OF LOVE
THE HERB FOR HAPPINESS

ONLY A DREAM
SAVED BY LOVE
LITTLE TONGUES OF FIRE
A CHIEFTAIN FINDS LOVE
THE LOVELY LIAR
THE PERFUME OF THE
   GODS
A KNIGHT IN PARIS
REVENGE IS SWEET
THE PASSIONATE
   PRINCESS
SOLITA AND THE SPIES
THE PERFECT PEARL
LOVE IS A MAZE
A CIRCUS FOR LOVE
THE TEMPLE OF LOVE
THE BARGAIN BRIDE
THE HAUNTED HEART
REAL LOVE OR FAKE
KISS FROM A STRANGER
A VERY SPECIAL LOVE
THE NECKLACE OF LOVE
A REVOLUTION OF LOVE
THE MARQUIS WINS
LOVE IS THE KEY
LOVE AT FIRST SIGHT
THE TAMING OF A
   TIGRESS
PARADISE IN PENANG
THE EARL RINGS
   A BELLE
THE QUEEN SAVES
   THE KING
NO DISGUISE FOR LOVE

Other Books by Barbara Cartland

THE ADVENTURER
AGAIN THIS RAPTURE
BARBARA CARTLAND'S
   BOOK OF BEAUTY
   AND HEALTH
BLUE HEATHER
BROKEN BARRIERS
THE CAPTIVE HEART
THE COIN OF LOVE
THE COMPLACENT WIFE
COUNT THE STARS
DESIRE OF THE HEART
DESPERATE DEFIANCE
THE DREAM WITHIN
ELIZABETHAN LOVER
THE ENCHANTING EVIL
ESCAPE FROM PASSION
FOR ALL ETERNITY
A GOLDEN GONDOLA
A HEART IS BROKEN
THE HIDDEN HEART

THE IRRESISTIBLE BUCK
THE KISS OF PARIS
THE KISS OF THE DEVIL
A KISS OF SILK
THE KNAVE OF HEARTS
THE LEAPING FLAME
A LIGHT TO THE HEART
LIGHTS OF LOVE
THE LITTLE PRETENDER
LOST ENCHANTMENT
LOVE AT FORTY
LOVE FORBIDDEN
LOVE IN HIDING
LOVE UNDER FIRE
THE MAGIC OF HONEY
METTERNICH THE
   PASSIONATE
   DIPLOMAT
MONEY, MAGIC AND
   MARRIAGE
NO HEART IS FREE

THE ODIOUS DUKE
OPEN WINGS
A RAINBOW TO HEAVEN
THE RELUCTANT BRIDE
THE SCANDALOUS LIFE
   OF KING CAROL
THE SMUGGLED HEART
A SONG OF LOVE
STARS IN MY HEART
STOLEN HALO
SWEET PUNISHMENT
THE THIEF OF LOVE
THIS TIME IT'S LOVE
TOUCH A STAR
TOWARDS THE STARS
THE UNKNOWN HEART
WE DANCED ALL NIGHT
THE WINGS OF ECSTASY
THE WINGS OF LOVE
WINGS ON MY HEART
WOMAN, THE ENIGMA

A NEW CAMFIELD NOVEL OF LOVE BY

BARBARA CARTLAND

No Disguise for Love

JOVE BOOKS, NEW YORK

NO DISGUISE FOR LOVE

A Jove Book / published by arrangement with
the author

PRINTING HISTORY
Jove edition / February 1991

ISBN: 0-515-10516-3

Jove Books are published by The Berkley Publishing Group,
200 Madison Avenue, New York, New York 10016.
The name "JOVE" and the "J" logo
are trademarks belonging to Jove Publications, Inc.

PRINTED IN THE UNITED STATES OF AMERICA

10 9 8 7 6 5 4 3 2 1

Author's Note

THE white slave traffic was flourishing in a horrifying manner at the end of the last century.

For years young girls had been taken out of the country to fill the harems of the Sultans and the Arab Chiefs.

Being dark, they particularly liked fair hair and fair-skinned women, and the English, Dutch, and the Germans were very much in demand.

When women were recruited from the Cities and became slaves to the men who owned them, they were broken in to their trade by cruelty and drugs.

This involved a procurer, who induced the girl of ill-fame; the importer or exporter, who took the girl to her destination; and thirdly, a man who in part lived on the immoral earnings of the woman.

Where the trade concerned the East, she remained a virgin until she was actually handed over to the man who had bought her.

Girls from the country who were the most gullible were enticed by advertisements like the following:

FINE POSITION for Young Lady. Independent. Not over 25, as companion to teach English, and travel on the Continent. Address with photo.

When the applicant was interviewed, usually by a charming good-class man who was very plausible, she was invariably attracted by the idea of going abroad and working for a distinguished family.

She was usually taken to her destination having no idea what would occur on arrival until it was too late.

chapter one

1874

THE Marquis of Calvadale looked across the Drawing-Room and saw that Lady Hester Sheldon was flirting outrageously with the French Ambassador.

He knew exactly why she was doing it, but it did not make him jealous, as she intended.

Instead, he was merely irritated.

If there was one thing he disliked, it was women, or men, who paraded their affections in public, or if they behaved, even when with close friends, without any reserve or what was called "propriety."

He was extremely fastidious and had pursued a great number of women when they were not pursuing him.

He had enjoyed the favours of most of the great Beauties of London.

He was, however, very circumspect and conscious of his ancestry.

However much he enjoyed himself, he was determined never to soil the family name.

He decided at this moment that his affair with Lady Hester was at an end.

She was indisputably one of the loveliest women in the whole of society.

At the same time, there was a wildness in her character which made the Marquis frown.

The daughter of the Earl of Battledon, Lady Hester had gone out to India to join her father, who was governor of Madras, when she was seventeen.

She had fallen head-over-heels in love with one of his *Aides-de-camp*.

Gordon Sheldon was a very handsome young man and undoubtedly breath-taking in his uniform.

Together with the background of Government House and the overwhelming beauty of India, he was irresistible.

Despite her father's misgivings, she had insisted on marrying Gordon Sheldon.

For two years they were more or less happy.

Then the Earl's five-year appointment was over and he returned to England.

After the splendours of Government House, Lady Hester was faced with a choice.

Should she go with her husband to live in married quarters at Aldershot or some other Army Head Quarters or return to her father's home in Norfolk?

She chose the latter, and from that moment the marriage was virtually over.

Gordon was posted overseas, and it was a relief to Hester when she learnt that he had been killed in a skirmish in Africa.

With Queen Victoria's eye upon her she dared not make her mourning any less than a year.

As soon as the gloomy months were over she came to London.

By this time her beauty had increased.

She had also learnt by constant practice the art of enslaving a man by a flicker of her eye-lashes.

She was the toast of all the London Clubs and of the Social World following the ball given for her by her father.

From that moment she was fêted, acclaimed, and pursued by every unmarried man in the *Beau Monde*.

Not unnaturally, it went to her head.

While she took several lovers, she refused a dozen proposals of marriage.

She decided coolly that none of the men in question were good enough for her.

It was inevitable that she should eventually meet the Marquis of Calvadale. When she did she knew at once he was exactly what she was looking for in a husband.

He bore a distinguished name and was extremely wealthy.

He was also a very handsome man with a charm which every woman he met found irresistible.

The difficulty was that the Marquis was determined not to marry.

He had seen too many unhappy marriages amongst his friends.

Therefore he had no intention of saddling himself with a wife simply because her blood happened to equal his, or because she would be approved of by his family as the Marchioness of Calvadale.

He was nearly thirty, but he laughed when his grandmother, his aunts, and his cousins begged him to marry.

"What is the hurry?" he had asked. "There is plenty of time for me to father any number of heirs, and frankly I prefer my freedom."

His freedom consisted of flitting from *Boudoir* to *Boudoir*.

He was also very successful as a race-horse owner, and he travelled a great deal.

Sometimes it was just for pleasure, at others it was at the request of the Secretary of State for Foreign Affairs or the Prime Minister.

He reasoned that it would spoil everything if he was forced to take a wife with him.

She would constrict his movements and would undoubtedly complain that she was being neglected.

It took Lady Hester nearly six months before the Marquis finally succumbed to her blandishments.

He would not have done so then if they had not been staying in a house-party which they both found exceedingly dull.

The Marquis had been inveigled into accepting an invitation for three days of pheasant-shooting in Huntingdonshire.

It had sounded as if it might be amusing. But when he arrived he found that most of his host's guests were much older than himself.

The rest were country folk with whom he had nothing in common.

He had made a mistake which he admitted to himself only an hour after his arrival.

The only redeeming feature was that Lady Hester Sheldon was there.

He had no idea that she had in fact gone to a great deal of trouble to be included in the house-party.

She had learnt he had been invited, and knew it was the opportunity that she had been waiting for.

It was a relief to the Marquis to find a "kindred spirit."

When they were in London they moved in the same circle of friends and could at least laugh at the same jokes.

He discovered that Lady Hester's bedroom was only a short distance from his down the corridor.

He thought to be with her would at least relieve what had been an extremely boring evening.

He was not mistaken.

He had suspected that Lady Hester would prove to be a tigress in bed.

In fact she was that, and a great deal more.

The following day, when the birds were high and there were a large number of them, he found the shooting enjoyable.

It was also a relief to find he was next to Lady Hester at dinner.

They talked together so exclusively that their partners on either side of them hardly received a word.

Soon after dinner they both retired to bed.

By the time they returned to London, Lady Hester had made up her mind that the Marquis would not escape her.

Because there was no one else in his life at that particular moment, they met each other every day.

Whenever it was possible, they spent the night together.

It annoyed Hester that he would not relax his principles and allow her to stay in his house.

If she dined with him, they did not go upstairs.

"What does it matter what the servants think?" she asked petulantly.

"Servants talk," he replied, "and I have to protect your reputation."

"What you are really thinking of is your own!" she snapped.

Then with a quick change of mood she moved nearer to him to say very softly:

"It would be quite easy, my dearest Favian, to ensure that nobody would be shocked by anything we do!"

The Marquis did not pretend to misunderstand her.

For a moment his eyes darkened.

Then he said:

"You are very attractive, Hester, but I somehow cannot imagine you in the role of wife and mother!"

"I do not see why not!" Hester argued.

As she saw the expression in his eyes, she knew she would never convince him with words.

Instead, she put her arms around his neck and drew his head down to hers.

"I love you," she said, "and nothing else is of any importance."

The Marquis kissed her.

As she clung to him he felt the fire burning inside him that was also burning in her.

At the same time, at the back of his mind he knew

this was not what he wanted for the rest of his life.

This evening, for a party given by Lady Beller, the Marquis had refused to pick up Hester on his way there.

"It is a mistake for us to arrive together," he had said.

"Oh, really, Favian, how can you be so strait-laced?" Hester taunted. "Everybody in London knows that we are always together. How can it possibly matter whether we arrive in two carriages or in one?"

"A number of people might assume that we came from the same house," the Marquis answered, "and there is nothing wrong with your carriage and horses."

"I swear you are becoming more and more like one of my maiden aunts!" Hester said angrily.

Then, as the Marquis rose to his feet, she knew she had made a mistake.

"Darling Favian, do not go!" she begged. "I have so much to say to you. I also want your kisses—I want them desperately!"

The Marquis disengaged himself from her clinging arms and reached the door.

"I will see you this evening," he answered.

"And will you take me home?" she enquired.

He knew exactly what that entailed, and hesitated.

"I will think about it," he replied.

Then he was gone and Lady Hester stamped her foot.

In her fury she deliberately dashed a pretty piece of Dresden china from the mantelpiece.

It broke into a thousand pieces.

"I will marry him, I will!" she told her reflection in the mirror.

At the same time, she had an uneasy feeling that the Marquis might escape her.

It was then she told herself she had been too easy.

What she must do, and she chided herself for not thinking of it before, was to make him jealous.

She took a great deal of trouble over her appearance that evening, determined to make herself look even lovelier than usual.

There was a new gown from the most expensive Dress-maker in Bond Street, whose models came from Paris.

Her Hair-dresser came to arrange her hair in a different style from how she had worn it before.

She applied creams and salves very cleverly to her face.

It was so subtly done that they were hardly noticeable.

They did, however, enhance the whiteness of her skin and the exquisite "Cupid's bow" shape of her lips.

"How can he resist me?" she asked when she was ready to leave.

As she walked down the stairs to where her carriage was waiting, she remembered that the Marquis was different from other men.

They had gone down on their knees before her, and swore that they would die if she refused them.

One man actually attempted to kill himself for love of her.

But however hard she tried, the Marquis remained the dominant member in their love-affair.

He inevitably had his own way.

Nothing she did could change him.

She was tortured daily by the thought that suddenly for some unexplained reason he might leave her.

But what man, she asked herself, is not jealous of his own possessions?

When she arrived at Lady Beller's house, which was not far from the Marquis's own Mansion in Grosvenor Square, Hester looked around her.

To her delight, she saw the French Ambassador was present.

She knew that his wife had just left for Paris.

He was delightfully French, and flirted amorously with every woman to whom he was attracted.

Hester moved across the room towards him.

Sitting down by his side, she looked up at him with an expression in her eyes that she knew was very inviting.

The Marquis was announced ten minutes later.

The French Ambassador was lifting Lady Hester's hand, from which she had removed her glove, to his lips.

The Marquis was unimpressed.

He continued to be irritated by Hester's behaviour for the rest of the evening.

He was not in the least jealous, because that was an emotion which he had never experienced.

He had never had any reason to be unsure of any woman he fancied.

He had never in his life made love to a woman who was not completely captivated by him.

They usually continued to be more and more infatuated until he bought the liaison to an end.

He was therefore just annoyed that Lady Hester was making an exhibition of herself.

He thought that the French Ambassador should be reminded that he was in London, not in Paris.

He was very fond of his hostess and enjoyed talking to her at dinner.

When the Gentlemen joined the Ladies after dinner, he sought out one of the men.

He particularly wanted to talk to him because he was an authority on Northern Africa.

He had recently written a book on Morocco.

"I enjoyed your book enormously!" the Marquis told him.

"You have really read it?" the Author asked.

"From cover to cover," the Marquis replied.

He was used to people being surprised that he should find time for reading.

His outdoor activities took up so much of his day, and nights were heavily booked!

Actually, any work of importance that was published he purchased automatically.

The huge Library in his country house was at present being extended in order to make room for his new collection.

He started to talk with appreciation of what he had read.

Finally the Author said:

"I know that you have travelled extensively, My Lord, but I do beg of you, when you have the time, to visit Fez. It is one of the most interesting of the great Moslem Cities, and I know you would find it as fascinating as I do."

"I shall certainly take your advice at the first opportunity," the Marquis replied.

It was at that point that his hostess took him away.

She wished to introduce him to somebody who she said was longing to meet him.

An hour later he decided he would go home.

He had not spoken a word to Hester.

When he rose to his feet, there were quite a number of people to whom he had to say good-night.

She was still with the Ambassador.

It was obvious to everybody in the room that they were absorbed in each other.

It appeared that as far as they were concerned, everybody else had ceased to exist.

In fact, the Marquis was aware that several *sotto voce* jokes were being made about their behaviour.

The somewhat mocking laughter that followed each of these made him feel ashamed for Hester.

He had no intention of saying good-night to her, nor of answering what he knew would be an invitation in her eyes.

Instead, he walked towards the door.

His hostess moved beside him, having a last word before he left.

Just as they reached the door, a very old lady, the Dowager Duchess of Cumbria, was getting to her feet.

"It is time for my bed, dear," she said in a somewhat quavering voice to Lady Beller.

"It has been a delight to have you here," Lady Beller replied. "I am just saying good-night to the Marquis of Calvadale, then I will come back to you."

The Dowager Duchess peered up at the Marquis,

and he realised she was very nearly blind.

"I have heard of you, young man!" she said. "Are you going to marry that pretty Lady Hester who I hear is a real handful?"

The Marquis stiffened.

Bending politely over the Dowager Duchess's hand, he replied:

"I am sure, Ma'am, you are aware of the saying that 'He travels fastest who travels alone'?"

The Dowager Duchess laughed.

"That is undoubtedly true, and if that is how you feel, then I should certainly think twice before becoming leg-shackled!"

The Marquis laughed before he said:

"I will take your advice, Ma'am!"

Before Lady Beller left him she said to him:

"You must not mind what the Dowager Duchess has just said. She belongs to a generation who express themselves far more frankly than we dare to do."

"I am not in the least offended," the Marquis replied, "and you know, as one of my oldest friends, that I have no intention of marrying anybody."

"I am sure you are right to make that decision," Lady Beller replied, "until you fall in love."

The Marquis smiled.

"Are you suggesting that I have never been in love?"

"I am, dear Favian," she answered. "Although you may not believe it, I do not think you have yet encountered the love that is completely irresistible and for too many men unobtainable."

She gave a little sigh before she added:

"When you do, you will know it is very, very different from what is 'Easy Come and Easy Go.' "

She spoke softly, and the Marquis knew she was in fact very fond of him.

What she was saying was part of a deep affection he never wished to lose.

He bent forward to kiss her on the cheek.

"Thank you," he said, "I know I can always rely on you."

"Always!"

As he walked across the hall to the front door, she returned to her other guests.

A footman helped him on with his evening-cloak and handed him his top hat.

Another flunkey asked:

"Shall I call your carriage, M'Lord?"

The Marquis shook his head.

"It is such a short distance to my home that I will walk there."

He stepped out into the night.

There was a moon, and it was easy for him to see his way.

He had only to walk the length of two streets before he would reach Grosvenor Square.

He set off thinking that the coolness of the night air was a relief after the warmth of the Drawing-Room with so many people in it.

As he walked down the empty street, the only sound being his own footsteps, he knew he was free of Hester.

He wondered if she would make a scene when she

realised he had finished with her.

He was used to tears and recriminations, which always irritated him.

At the same time, they made him feel somewhat guilty.

He told himself over and over again that women who were promiscuous, and certainly those who deceived their husbands, deserved no consideration or sympathy.

Yet when a woman cried because he was leaving her, he was always tempted to take her into his arms and comfort her.

But he knew that would only make things worse than they were already.

The best thing he could do, he thought, was not to see Hester again.

Unfortunately that was impossible if he remained in London.

And if he went to the country she would undoubtedly follow him.

"What shall I do?" he asked himself.

At that moment he was walking down South Audley Street.

As he passed one of the largest houses, the door opened and a young woman ran out into the street.

"Stop, thief!" she cried.

He had just passed the house, but he turned back to see what was happening.

The light from the hall behind her shone on his face, and she exclaimed:

"Oh . . . I am sorry! I thought you were somebody else."

She was young and very pretty, although he thought there was something slightly odd about her.

"Have you been burgled?" he asked.

"No, but a man has left . . . me and taken with . . . him something very valuable."

"A man?" the Marquis asked. "Do you mean someone you know?"

The girl gave a little sob and made a gesture with her hand.

"I have been . . . a fool . . . an absolute . . . fool!" she said. "And now . . . I do not know . . . what to do . . . about it."

"Can I help?" the Marquis asked.

She looked at him as if it were an effort, because she was thinking of something else.

Then she exclaimed:

"You are the Marquis of Calvadale!"

The Marquis smiled.

"So you know me?"

"No, but my brother is always talking about . . . you and . . . your horses. He is Sir Ian Warrington."

The Marquis remembered a young man he had encountered on a number of race-courses.

"I have met your brother," he said, "and perhaps I can help you, if you tell me about your loss."

The girl looked up and down the street which was empty.

"He may have gone a long way by now," she said, "and . . . I suppose I shall not be able to catch him. What . . . shall I do?"

"Suppose you tell me about it?" the Marquis suggested.

"Yes . . . of course . . . although I do not think . . . anyone can help me . . . but come inside. We cannot talk . . . out here."

"No, of course not," the Marquis agreed.

The girl went up the steps in front of him, and he followed her.

There was no footman in the hall.

She shut the door behind them.

Without speaking, she led the way into an attractively furnished Sitting-Room.

It was lit by several oil-lamps.

The Marquis could see there were fine pictures on the walls and the furniture was in good taste and luxurious.

The girl then asked:

"May I offer you . . . something to drink? I cannot think he can have drugged anything but what . . . was in . . . my glass."

"Drugged?" the Marquis exclaimed. "What are you saying?"

The girl hesitated and he said:

"I want nothing to drink, thank you. But if it is possible, I will try to help you. Where is your brother?"

"He has gone to a race-meeting in the country," the girl said. "One of my relatives is staying with me, but she is asleep and I do not want to . . . disturb her."

"No, of course not," the Marquis agreed.

He sat down in a chair.

Then as he looked at the girl in the light he saw to his surprise that she was heavily made-up.

There was rouge on her cheeks, mascara on her eye-lashes.

Undoubtedly her lips were very much redder than nature intended them to be.

Then he saw that the gown she was wearing was flamboyant and her hair was arranged in a style not usually worn by a Lady.

As if she were aware that he was staring at her questioningly, she said:

"I suppose you are . . . surprised at . . . the way I . . . look, and that is . . . the reason why I am in . . . such a . . . mess."

"Start from the beginning," the Marquis said. "First of all, what is your name? Is it the same as your brother's?"

"Yes, it is, and my Christian name is Narda, which means 'joyous.' But I certainly do not feel any joy at the moment."

"Then of course I must ask why not?" the Marquis said.

The girl gave a little sigh and sank down on the hearth-rug.

Her full skirt flowed out on either side of her.

"I have been such . . . a fool," she said, "and now, I suppose, I must . . . pay for . . . it!"

"Tell me your story," the Marquis suggested, "and perhaps between us we can find a solution."

"I think that would be . . . impossible!" Narda exclaimed. "It all happened because some friends of whom Mama, if she were alive, would not have approved, invited me to a party."

"And why would your mother not have approved?"

"Because they are rather 'dashing,' I suppose you could say 'vulgar' people, whom Ian, my brother, met on the race-course.

"And he introduced them to you?" the Marquis said.

"Ian brought them home one evening for a drink, and after they had gone he told me I was to have nothing to do with them in the future, and that he had made a mistake in letting them meet me in the first place."

"He was trying to protect you," the Marquis remarked.

"I know," Narda said, "but I met one of the girls again at my Dress-maker's. She was really very nice and we became friends."

She spoke a little defiantly, as if she expected the Marquis to criticise her.

When he said nothing, she went on:

"I met Beris there several times because we were both having gowns fitted. Then two days ago she told me about a party they were giving to-night."

"A party you should not have gone to," the Marquis remarked.

"I knew that," Narda agreed, "but Ian had gone away and I was desperately bored with Aunt Edith. Also, it was a challenge."

"Tell me about the party."

"Beris told me that the party was being given for a Moroccan Sheikh who had come to England to buy horses. She said he was very attractive and thought it would amuse me to meet him."

Narda hesitated a moment before she said, again somewhat defiantly:

"Of course I wanted to meet a Sheikh! I had read about them, and I have always been fascinated by stories of Africa. Then Beris said to me:

" 'It would be fun for you to come, but you cannot come as yourself.'

" 'What do you mean by that?' I asked.

" 'Well, some of the guests who are invited are 'Gaiety Girls,' and I am sure the Sheikh will find them amusing. Everyone else is much older than us, of course, and very sophisticated.' "

Narda paused.

The Marquis, who was listening intently, thought she looked at him pleadingly before she begged:

"Try to . . . understand! I know it was . . . wrong of me, but I have always . . . enjoyed dressing-up and I have also fancied myself as . . . an actress."

"So what did you do?" he asked.

"I . . . I went looking like a . . . Gaiety Girl . . . at least . . . I thought I did."

The Marquis realised that that accounted for the make-up on her face and the mascara on her eyelashes.

"Beris knows a woman," Narda went on, "who disposes of the gowns that the Gaiety Girls sell after wearing them so often that they cannot be seen in them again."

She looked down at the dress and said:

"This is one of them."

"I thought it was somewhat flamboyant for somebody as young as you!" the Marquis remarked.

"The whole point is that I was trying . . . not to look . . . so young!" Narda replied. "Beris did my hair for me and she told me it was exactly how some of the Gaiety Girls were wearing theirs. I had an osprey in it but I pulled it off when I came home."

"That was when you came back here with the Sheikh," the Marquis said.

"I know it was very, very stupid of me to ask him in," Narda said, "but actually he insisted on having a drink."

"And what did he steal from you?" the Marquis asked.

"I can hardly believe he did it when he is so rich," Narda replied. "The gown I am wearing is rather . . . low in the front . . . so I decided to put on a . . . necklace that belonged to my mother, and which Ian . . . treasures more than . . . anything else we possess."

"What does it look like?" the Marquis asked.

"It was a necklace that my grandfather was given many years ago by an Indian Maharajah and which is not only very valuable but also unique."

She gave what was almost a sob as she said:

"Ian adores it, and although a number of people have tried to buy it from him, he has always sworn that he will never part with it, and his son will inherit it when he has one."

"What is it like?" the Marquis asked again.

"It is a very elaborate piece of jewellery made of large rubies, emeralds, and diamonds. It could only have come from the East, and the stones are outstanding. However hard I tried . . . I could . . . never replace . . . them."

Narda was very near to tears, and the Marquis said:

"You were wearing it when you came back here with the Sheikh. What is he like?"

"Tall, dark, and really very handsome!" Narda replied. "He was younger than I expected, and one could imagine him riding magnificent horses across the desert."

The Marquis thought cynically that like all women she believed that Arab Sheikhs were romantic Romeos.

He had found them ruthless Rulers of their small communities with invariably a mercenary streak where anything to do with money was concerned.

"So despite the competition, you were a success with the Sheikh!" he said.

"I was, and it was surprising," Narda replied. "I meant only to look at him. I never expected him even to speak to me."

The Marquis was perceptively aware that it was her youth that had attracted the Arab.

Despite the manner in which she had tried to hide it, she looked both young and innocent.

"So after you talked with him and, I expect, danced with him, he brought you home."

"He insisted upon doing so. He sent away my carriage and we came back in his."

"So he has a carriage!" the Marquis said quickly.

"When we reached here he told the coachman not to wait. I thought it was because he was staying quite near."

The Marquis thought the Sheikh had other reasons, but he merely said:

"Tell me exactly what happened."

"We came into this room," Narda said, "and as there is a grog-tray standing in the corner I asked him what he would like to drink. He hesitated for a moment, and looked at me in a strange way which made me feel . . . rather shy."

She did not tell the Marquis that she thought that there was a fire in the Sheikh's eyes which made her feel a little afraid.

It might have been a trick of the light.

He had looked into her face.

Then his eyes had gone to her necklace.

In a different tone of voice from what he had used when they were in the carriage together, he had said:

"Tell me about your necklace. I am sure it comes from the East."

"Yes, it does," Narda replied. "It was given to my grandfather by the Maharajah to whom he did a great service. My family is very proud of it, but this is the first time I have worn it."

She did not add that because it was so large, she had thought it was the type of necklace a Gaiety Girl would wear.

Her mother had always said the same thing because the necklace was so very flashy.

"It is certainly very beautiful!" the Sheikh exclaimed. "Now, sit down and let me get a drink for you, and one for myself. I cannot allow anyone so lovely to wait on me!"

Narda had thought it was rather touching.

She knew in the East it was the women who always waited on the men.

She thought that Beris would also think it amusing.

She therefore walked to one of the chairs at the side of the hearth.

She watched the Sheikh as he poured some wine into a glass.

He started to fill another, but she said:

"I would rather have lemonade. There is a small jug of it there."

The Sheikh had moved as he looked for the lemonade so that she could only see his back.

She saw that his hair was very dark.

She thought if he were in his own country, it would be covered.

He seemed to take a long time filling the glass.

Then he came across the room with one in each hand.

He handed her the glass of lemonade, and as she took it from him she thought she was in fact rather thirsty.

"I think we should drink a toast," the Sheikh said.

He raised his glass and because Narda thought it was expected of her, she raised hers.

"May Fate or your Karma bring you happiness," the Sheikh said, "and you must repeat that after me."

A little shyly Narda did as she was told.

Then he said:

"Now you must drink everything in your glass or it will be unlucky."

She raised her glass to her lips.

She found there was not so much lemonade in it as she expected and drank it down.

"It was . . . then," she said in a low voice to the Marquis, "that I felt . . . a darkness creeping up . . .

from the floor . . . and for a moment . . . or it might have . . . been longer . . . I knew . . . nothing."

"He had drugged you!" the Marquis finished.

"If it was a drug, it was a very strange one," Narda said, "because when I opened my eyes I did not realise anything had happened, except that now he was . . . not there. I looked round the room, thinking he could hardly have . . . left without saying . . . good-bye."

She made a little gesture as if to express her surprise.

"As I rose to my feet I saw my empty glass where it had fallen to the floor. It had not broken and I pushed it to one side, still thinking the Sheikh had behaved in a strange manner."

She paused before she said:

"I walked to the door, thinking perhaps he was in the hall. There is a large mirror on one of the walls, and when I saw my reflection in it I realised that the necklace had gone!"

"You are quite certain it was round your neck when you came back from the party?"

"Yes, of course, because the Sheikh had talked about it."

"Yes—I remember," the Marquis said. "Go on!"

"I could not . . . believe it had . . . happened," Narda said. "I went back into the Sitting-Room to see if it had fallen down beside my chair."

The Marquis heard the horror in her voice as she went on:

"Then I saw the Sheikh's glass where he had put it down on a side-table. At that moment I knew he had stolen it! I ran to the hall and out through the front door, thinking perhaps I would see him going down the street, but there was only . . . you."

"And that was how we met," the Marquis said quietly.

"But . . . what can I do . . . tell me . . . what can I do? Ian will never . . . forgive me for . . . losing his necklace . . . and how can the Sheikh be . . . nothing but a . . . common thief?"

"Those questions can be answered only if one is in his own country," the Marquis said. "Do you know where that is?"

"At least I know that," Narda replied. "He comes from Fez. They told me he has a large house there that is almost a palace, as well as a Kasbah in the desert."

The Marquis thought that he might have guessed that Fez would be the answer.

"I think after what you have told me I can help you," he said to Narda, "because quite shortly, in fact almost at once, I am going to Fez!"

chapter two

IT seemed to the Marquis as if Fate were interfering in his life and there was no use in fighting against it.

The previous day before luncheon he had called at the Foreign Office.

This was in response to a note he had received from Lord Derby, the Secretary of State for Foreign Affairs.

In it he said that he wished to see him as soon as possible.

When the Marquis walked into Lord Derby's office, he said, before the Minister could speak:

"If, My Lord, you have something ghastly for me to do like crossing the desert bare-foot or climbing the Himalayas, the answer is 'No'!"

Lord Derby laughed.

He had known the Marquis for many years.

He thought as he came into the room that he was

growing more handsome every time he saw him.

"Sit down, Favian," he said, "and listen to what I have to tell you."

"That is what frightens me!" the Marquis retorted. "Whenever I listen to you I find myself doing something I have no wish to do, but I am hypnotised into accepting your absurd and usually dangerous missions!"

Lord Derby laughed again.

Then he said in a serious tone:

"I think you will find what I have to tell you interesting, and I assure you it does not involve climbing the Himalayas."

"What about the desert?" the Marquis asked suspiciously.

"It is only background music!" Lord Derby replied, and now the Marquis laughed.

Then Lord Derby turned over some papers on his desk and said:

"What I am going to tell you concerns the North West of Africa, and you will not be surprised to learn that it involves the White Slave Traffic."

The Marquis groaned.

"Not that old story," he protested. "I have been hearing about it for years, and personally, I think it is very exaggerated."

"The majority of the Members of Parliament would agree with you," Lord Derby replied, "but the Prime Minister is rather concerned, and so am I."

"Why?" the Marquis asked.

"To put you in the picture," Lord Derby said, "you know that after many years of confusion and near-anarchy in North Africa things are at last settling down quietly in Morocco."

"I know that your prime interest," the Marquis said, "is to ensure that the Southern Shore of the Straits of Gibraltar should not be controlled by a rival European power."

"That is correct," Lord Derby agreed, "and that is why Britain is supporting the independence of Morocco and has pressed for reforms."

"And I suppose you think you are going to get them," the Marquis said a little mockingly.

He was well aware of the trouble and difficulties that had been created in Morocco by the rivalry between France and Spain.

Fourteen years ago peace had been restored.

This was because the British Government had made it clear it would not accept a permanent Spanish occupation of the Moroccan Coast.

"Things are changing for the better," Lord Derby was saying. "The new Sultan, Mulay el-Hassan, who succeeded last year, is a man of strong character."

The Marquis did not speak, and after a moment Lord Derby went on:

"Our British Representative, Sir John Drummond Hay, thinks highly of him and, as you know, Sir John has made certain of our influence in the country, especially as regards Trade."

"Money always talks!" the Marquis said dryly.

"I agree with you," Lord Derby replied, "and we are very concerned that nothing should disrupt the friendly relations which now exist between Britain and the new Sultan."

28

"And you think that might be endangered by the White Slave Traffic?" the Marquis enquired.

He thought as he spoke that it seemed impossible, that Lord Derby was "making a mountain out of a mole-hill."

There had always been a certain amount of trouble in Moslem countries.

Wild rumours of white women being kidnapped from England and other European countries had been current for centuries.

The women were shut up in Harems in Turkey or North Africa from which they could never escape.

The subject had become a favourite plot with Novelists.

However, a great number of people were sceptical about it and believed the traffic was not half as prevalent as was alleged.

"I assure you," Lord Derby said, reading the doubt on the Marquis's face, that we have made every possible enquiry. But I admit it is very difficult to prove that anything on a large scale is taking place."

"And yet you really think it is?" the Marquis questioned.

"As you know, Moslems are permitted four wives and unlimited concubines," Lord Derby answered, "and there have recently been a great number of women reputed to being Moslem wives travelling from England to Morocco."

The Marquis thought it would be very difficult to prove if the bride was unwilling.

But he did not speak, and Lord Derby went on:

"There have also been a number of ships carrying cargo which our Customs Officers suspect is not entirely what it purports to be."

"What do you mean by that?" the Marquis asked.

Lord Derby sighed.

"Ships can have hiding-places built into them, and coffins with drugged women confined in them are very difficult to investigate without causing trouble."

He frowned as he continued:

"There are hundreds of different ways by which young women, and of course the Arabs like them very young, can be shipped out of the country without our being aware of it."

"And you really think this is going on on a large scale?" the Marquis asked.

"Sir John Drummond Hay is very eager that nothing should upset our friendly relations with the new Sultan, but you know as well as I do, Favian, that if the 'Do-gooders' get to hear of this, there will be a tremendous outcry which will undoubtedly annoy the Moslems."

"Why, in particular?"

"Because," Lord Derby said, "the traffic which is alleged to be taking place is mainly in Fez, which you know is holy to the Moslems. They would certainly resent a scandal which will reflect on the sanctity and dignity of their City."

"I understand what you are saying," the Marquis agreed, "and of course we all know the Moslems are very touchy where anything concerns their Holy Cities like Marrakesh, Rabat, Meknés, and of course Fez."

He settled himself more comfortably in his chair before he asked:

"What are you asking me to do? To try to snatch

some drugged girl from an Arab's arms? I can imagine nothing more conducive to having a knife through my heart!"

He was speaking jokingly, but Lord Derby said:

"What I am asking you to do, Favian, is what you have done so often for me in the past—to find out the truth and to ascertain whether the stories we have been told are exaggerated or not."

"And then?"

"Once we have a pointer in the right direction, I am quite certain Sir John can deal with it, or persuade the Sultan that what is happening is not for his country's good."

"I can see this quiet but ambitious little idea of yours," the Marquis replied, "will land me in serious trouble. I shall certainly make my will before I leave!"

Lord Derby laughed.

"I expect you have done that innumerable times before, but always you have come up smiling, having been of tremendous help to the Foreign Office."

He leaned across the desk before he said:

"All I am asking, Favian, is for you to go to Fez, when you have the time, look around, be charming to a few of its most illustrious citizens, and find out in your own inimitable way exactly what is going on."

"Flattery will get you nowhere, My Lord!" the Marquis gibed. "I have no wish to go to Fez at the moment. I am enjoying myself in London!"

"She is certainly very lovely!" Lord Derby remarked. "But I have never known any of your *affaires de coeur* to last very long, because you quickly become bored."

"Now you are being insulting!" the Marquis retorted. "Let me make it quite clear that at the moment I am not at all bored."

Lord Derby made an expressive gesture with his hand before he said:

"In which case, I am quite prepared to wait until you are!"

Then the Marquis was laughing again, and Lord Derby rose from his desk.

He opened a door of one of the cabinets in the room.

Inside there were wine glasses and decanters.

"I feel I must drink to your success in what I have asked you to do," he said.

"You know full well that I have not yet agreed to do what you asked," the Marquis parried.

"You have never failed me yet!" Lord Derby replied. "And I refuse to anticipate a first time."

He poured some wine into a glass and carried it to the Marquis.

"I want you to try this," he said. "It is a very special vintage which the French Ambassador brought me last month. As there are only three bottles so far in this country, I have been keeping it for a special occasion."

"Now you are starting to soften me up," the Marquis said. "I know your methods only too well."

He was smiling as he spoke.

Then as he sipped the wine he exclaimed:

"Excellent! I will certainly send an invitation to the French Ambassador in the hope that he is as generous to me as he has been to you!"

Lord Derby raised his glass.

"To you, Favian!" he said. "May you add yet another success to the secret file to which I am the only person to have the key."

Now the Marquis saw the astonishment in Narda's eyes when he told her he was going to Fez.

As he did so the conversation with Lord Derby and the delicious bouquet of his wine flashed through his mind.

'It is no use fighting against Fate!' he told himself.

First Lord Derby had begged him to visit the Holy City.

Then the author at dinner had recommended it.

Thirdly, there was this cry for help from a young woman for whom he had a great deal of sympathy.

He knew only too well how attractive a Sheikh from Morocco must have seemed to a very young girl.

She had dug a pit of destruction for herself.

An innocent little *débutante* had gone to the party pretending to be a sophisticated actress.

She was extremely pretty, in fact; 'lovely' was the right word.

The Marquis could understand why the Sheikh had sought her out of all the other women in the party.

Of course he had intended to seduce her.

It was doubtful, once he was in the house, whether she would have been able to defend herself or call for assistance.

It had been a crazy action on her part to have let him in.

But it was unlikely she would have been able to prevent him anyway from virtually forcing his way in.

The Marquis could see very clearly what had happened.

She was the youngest girl at the party and she would certainly have been the most beautiful.

What Arab could ask for more?

Narda had remembered how he had looked at her in a manner which made her feel shy before he noticed the necklace.

As it was Eastern and also very valuable, it was inevitable that the Sheikh should have been attracted by it.

More attracted to it than to a girl who was heavily made-up and dressed as if she were not a virgin, which an Arab would prefer.

The Marquis was aware that in the Arab World there were innumerable drugs which worked in dozens of different ways.

He had heard of the one which Narda had described.

It rendered anyone who took it immediately unconscious, but they recovered very quickly and without any side-effects.

He guessed that a man like the Sheikh would find it so convenient that he would carry it with him.

It would enable him to seduce any pretty woman, to render any rival in Trade unconscious so that he could read his business papers without his being aware he had done so.

This was one of the drugs which could be of inestimable value to a man who was curious about another man's secrets.

"What I have to do," the Marquis declared, "is to

find out more about Sheikh Rachid Shriff and see if there is any chance of retrieving the necklace."

"Are you really going to Fez?" Narda was asking.

Now the despondent expression in her eyes had been replaced by a little gleam of hope.

"I have some business there," the Marquis said, "and I will certainly do what I can to try and find out what has happened to your necklace. Did the Sheikh say when he was returning home?"

"He said he was leaving almost at once. He was telling everybody at the party how much he had enjoyed being in London, and in the carriage he said to me:

" 'When I leave to-morrow I will be thinking of what an enjoyable party this has been and how delightful it was to meet you.' "

"Have you any idea where he is staying?" the Marquis asked.

Narda shook her head.

"He just said he was taking me home because he was going in my direction."

The Marquis thought he might be in any of the Hotels in that part of London.

Alternatively, the Sheikh might be staying with friends.

It would be hopeless at this time of the night to try to discover his whereabouts.

The only thing he could do would be to make enquiries about him when he reached Fez.

"When will you be going to Morocco?" Narda asked.

"Perhaps to-morrow or the next day," the Marquis replied.

"Then . . . please may I come . . . with you?"

The Marquis looked at her in astonishment.

"No, of course not!"

"But . . . if I do not do so . . . how can you . . . possibly find the necklace . . . and if the Sheikh . . . does not wish to . . . part with it . . . he might . . . give you an . . . imitation . . . or just any Oriental . . . piece of rubbish."

"If you draw me a picture of it, I am sure I will not be taken in," the Marquis replied.

"You might be," Narda argued, "and I would . . . like to . . . come with . . . you."

"No doubt you would," the Marquis replied, "but you have got yourself into a great deal of trouble already by doing what is unconventional. I therefore suggest that in future you behave in a more circumspect manner, as your mother would expect you to do."

There was silence for a moment.

Then Narda said:

"You know I . . . have to go . . . to Fez . . . so please . . . be sensible and let me . . . "

"Now, what do you mean by that?" the Marquis asked sharply.

"I mean that in order to save the necklace . . . for my brother, I must go to Fez . . . myself. I only . . . hope that I can meet you . . . there."

"This is utterly ridiculous!" the Marquis exclaimed. "Of course you cannot go to Fez alone. Who could you take with you?"

"I could take my lady's-maid, but she would be more trouble than she is worth, so I had much better go on my own."

The Marquis rose and stood in front of the fire-place.

"Now, listen, Miss Warrington," he said, "you are very young and, if you will forgive me for saying so, very foolish! You have got yourself into a nasty mess, and quite frankly, I think you were very lucky to have escaped as easily as you have."

"What do you . . . mean by . . . that?" Narda asked.

The Marquis was about to explain, then he thought it would be a mistake.

Instead, he said:

"What you have to do now is to behave as if nothing has happened, and leave everything in my hands."

"Do you really think I could do that?" Narda asked. "I am desperate, completely desperate, about the necklace. My brother will be so furious when he finds out that he will send me to the country and I shall have nothing to do but cry."

"Perhaps your brother will not learn the truth before I return, as I hope to do, with the necklace in my hand," the Marquis said.

"But you will never find the Sheikh . . . I know you will never . . . find him!" Narda protested. "How will you travel to Fez?"

"In my yacht," the Marquis replied. "It will be quicker and more comfortable than any other way, and I will try to get back as soon as possible."

He thought as he spoke that was what he wanted himself.

He was quite certain he would be able to find out

all Lord Derby required within a few days of being in Fez.

He had quite a number of contacts in the Arab world who he knew would help him.

"I am coming with you whatever you say," Narda declared. "It will not be easy for you to find the Sheikh. He might have assumed a different name, but I should recognise him however cleverly he disguises himself."

"Now, listen," the Marquis said, "you are not coming with me, and there is therefore no point in discussing it."

"Very well," Narda said, "I shall go to Gibraltar by train, or perhaps take a ship going there."

"You cannot make such a journey alone!"

"That is what you are forcing me to do. You can hardly expect me to tell my brother what I am doing, and my aunt, who is upstairs, is always ill. She would be concerned that such a long journey would kill her!"

"You must have other friends," the Marquis said.

"They are in the country, and they never travel. As I have already told you, because I have only just come to London, I have very few friends here."

The Marquis's lips tightened.

"It is a sad story," he said at length, "but there is nothing I can do about it. You must stay here until I return!"

"I will meet you in Fez!" Narda said obstinately.

The Marquis knew that travelling either by ship or by rail without being properly escorted and chaperoned, she would soon be in far greater trouble than she was already.

She was far too pretty, too young, and too innocent.

It was only by a miracle in the form of an Oriental necklace that she had been saved from the Sheikh, something which apparently had not yet occurred to her.

Any young girl, any older woman for that matter, travelling alone would find herself the prey of innumerable men.

There were plenty who had nothing better to do than look for such "pickings."

Because he knew he had to be very firm, the Marquis said:

"If you take up that attitude, I am going to refuse to help you in any way. We met purely by chance, and I have offered you my assistance on my own terms. If you refuse, there is nothing further I can do!"

He spoke very assertively.

It usually made anyone to whom he was speaking either apologise or cringe in front of him.

Narda did neither.

She merely laughed.

"Now you are definitely trying to frighten me," she said. "You know as well as I do that you are too much of a gentleman to walk away and leave me to my fate!"

For a moment the Marquis did not reply, and she went on:

"When you get to Fez you will try to find the necklace, but the Sheikh will deceive you in one way or another. I know he will!"

She put her hand on his arm and said:

39

"I promise you I will be no trouble if I can come in your yacht. You will not even know I am there unless you want to, but . . . I will be very frightened if I have to make the journey alone."

"It is quite impossible!" the Marquis said.

"Nothing is impossible," Narda answered. "I will leave a letter telling my brother that I have gone away to stay with friends."

She stared at the Marquis, thinking he was going to argue, and went on quietly:

"Anyway, he may not be back for another fortnight, as he has been asked after the race-meeting to stay with some people in Doncaster."

"I cannot possibly be back in a fortnight!" the Marquis said sharply.

"I assure you, Ian will not worry about me, and he is not worrying now. If he had been in London, I would not have gone to the party."

This was certainly logical, and the Marquis announced:

"You cannot come with me unchaperoned, and I have no intention of taking a party with me—in fact, I dislike yacht parties of any kind!"

This was true.

When for whatever reason he went abroad in his yacht, he always preferred to be on his own, and certainly when he was on a mission of any importance.

It was a nuisance to have his friends asking questions as to where he was going and why.

It was tiresome to have to organise entertainment for them if he was dining with the Foreign Minister.

It was difficult to meet one of his strange contacts, often in disguise.

"It would be a great mistake for anyone to know I was with you," Narda admitted, "but since I am so unimportant, there is no reason why anyone should be aware that I am in your yacht."

This was certainly true.

But it was impossible, the Marquis knew, to have a *débutante* travelling alone with him.

If it was discovered, he would be forced by her relatives and public opinion to make an honest woman of her.

Of one thing he was certain: he had no wish to marry Narda Warrington.

As if she had read his thoughts, Narda said:

"I could be in disguise. Perhaps I could sign on as an assistant in your galley. Actually I am quite a good cook!"

"I would not think of including you amongst my crew!" the Marquis said sharply.

"Then perhaps you could say I am a relative who has been very ill, and you thought the sea air would help me on my way to recovery."

"The trouble with you," the Marquis said irritably, "is that you are too imaginative. If you had not gone to that party pretending to be a Gaiety Girl, you would not be in the fix you are in now!"

"It was really rather fun!" Narda retorted with a rebellious little flash in her eye. "Men said things in front of me that they never would have said if they had known I was a society *débutante*. In fact, I think some of the other women were a little jealous!"

"Forget you ever went to it!" the Marquis said sternly. "And try to remember that you are a Lady."

Narda gave a little exclamation.

"Now you are talking just like my aunt Edith! She is forever saying, 'A *Lady* always wears her gloves!' 'A *Lady* does not hold her skirt too high!' 'A *Lady* walks gracefully and does not run!' I am sick to death of being a *Lady*!"

"I hardly think you have given it a fair trial," the Marquis said sarcastically.

"I have . . . I really have!" Narda protested. "And since it has . . . proved a . . . failure, I might . . . just as well be myself and enjoy it."

"If by that you mean that you still want to come on my yacht—forget it!" the Marquis said.

"Very well," Narda sighed, "I will meet you in Fez. Perhaps you would be good enough to tell me in what port you will anchor your yacht, and where in Fez you will be staying."

"I cannot go on saying over and over again that I will not take you with me!" the Marquis exclaimed.

"And I am tired of saying that it is something I intend to do!" Narda retorted.

"I shall send for your brother!" the Marquis said firmly.

"I have not told you where he is, and it would be difficult for you to find him. Anyway, I think you are being horrible and most unsporting."

Unexpectedly he laughed.

"You are hopeless!" he said. "Completely and utterly hopeless, and I wash my hands of you."

"At the same time," Narda said in a small voice,

"you . . . will take . . . me with you . . . to Fez?"

The Marquis walked across the room and back again.

He was wondering what he could do about this impulsive child.

He was certain that if he did not take her with him, she would in fact attempt to make the journey on her own.

He knew it would be on his conscience for the rest of his life if he allowed her to do that.

He had only to look at her to realise how young and unspoilt she was.

He was quite certain she had never been kissed.

It made him shudder to think what might have happened to her to-night had not the Sheikh's greed exceeded his amorous intentions.

"I have to do something about her!" he told himself.

Narda was watching him.

When he had walked back to where she was standing, he said:

"I will try and think of a solution to this problem."

"The only solution is for me to come with you on your yacht," Narda replied. "And as I am afraid you will slip away without telling me, I will come to your house at nine o'clock to-morrow morning with my luggage."

"How do you know where my house is?" the Marquis enquired.

"I was walking in Grosvenor Square two days ago when I saw CALVADALE HOUSE written over the door and thought it was very impressive."

"It would be a great mistake for you to come to my house," the Marquis argued. "I promise you I will not 'slip away,' as you suspect, and I will try to think how I can help you."

Her eyes lit up for a moment.

Then she asked:

"Can I . . . trust you?"

"Most people do," the Marquis replied, "especially when I give them my word."

Narda smiled.

"I told you you were a Gentleman and a sportsman, and I promise I will behave very, very well. I never get sea-sick, however rough the sea may be."

"I have to think of some way of getting you to Fez," the Marquis said. "Until I do, you will wait here and not do anything rash like coming to my house and making a scene."

"I will make a scene only if I find you have gone without me," Narda retorted.

The Marquis pressed his lips together.

"You are an exceedingly tiresome young woman!" he told her. "If I had any sense I would leave you to your fate and, what is more, certainly not go to Fez!"

He thought Narda would look suitably rebuked by his words.

Instead, she said:

"I know you are going to help me because you said you would, and you have just told me that you never break your word!"

The Marquis thought he had been 'hoisted by his own petard.'

Without speaking, he walked towards the door.

Narda ran after him.

"You promise you will come first thing to-morrow and tell me what you have planned? I shall pack everything to-night that I will need, just in case you wish to leave early."

The Marquis thought there was no use talking about it anymore.

Of all the turnip-brained, pig-headed women he had ever met, this child was the worst!

He swung his evening-cape over his shoulders.

He picked up his hat from where he had left it when he entered the house.

Narda opened the door for him.

"I am very, very . . . lucky to have met you," she said. "Thank you, thank you, for saying you . . . will help me!"

The Marquis knew she was only "rubbing it in" that he had said he never broke his word.

"Good-night!" he said briefly as he went down the steps.

He started to walk towards Grosvenor Square.

He was aware that Narda was watching him go from the doorway.

He reached the end of South Audley Street and turned towards his house.

He looked back.

She was standing where he had left her, and she waved her hand.

The Marquis was swearing beneath his breath as he walked on.

chapter three

THE Marquis awoke early, and as soon as he came downstairs for breakfast, he said to the Butler:

"Tell Major Ashley I want him."

He knew that his Secretary, who was a very unusual one, would be in his office.

A few minutes later Major Ashley came into the room.

He was a good-looking man.

But in a dangerous encounter in which both he and the Marquis had been involved when they were in the Army he had lost an eye.

Because the Marquis had been lucky enough to escape unscathed, he had felt in a way responsible for the man who had been his Senior Officer.

A month or so after Major Ashley was invalided out of the Army, the Marquis inherited his title.

He then asked the Major if he could come and work for him as his Secretary.

Major Ashley, who was nine years older than the Marquis, jumped at the opportunity.

It proved to be one of the most successful decisions the Marquis had ever made.

The Major had a genius for organisation.

Where the Marquis was concerned, he was not so much a Secretary as a Comptroller.

First he took over everything appertaining to the Marquis's private life.

Soon he was administering the Marquis's various estates.

He managed his racing-stables, his Hunting Lodge, his grouse moor, and everything else that was part of his great possessions.

The two men got on admirably.

The Major was the only person in whom the Marquis confided.

When they were in the Army they had both been involved in what amounted to espionage.

It was therefore a great relief to the Marquis to be able to discuss this secret part of his life with the Major.

When he undertook missions on behalf of the Queen or the Foreign Secretary, he could ask the Major's advice.

Whether it was before or after action took place, the Major would understand exactly what he was talking about.

Now, as Major Ashley came into the Breakfast-Room and the servants withdrew, the Marquis said:

"Sit down, Brian. I have something to tell you."

The Major did as he was told.

He drew up a chair to the table and sat so that he was facing the Marquis.

The black patch over one eye gave him a raffish appearance, not unlike that of a Pirate.

Over six feet tall and broad-shouldered, he still carried himself like a soldier.

His air of authority was very apparent to all those with whom he came into contact.

"What has happened, My Lord?" he asked.

He insisted upon addressing the Marquis formally in spite of the fact they were such close friends.

He had explained why when the Marquis protested.

"I am employed by you and I therefore have to set an example to those beneath me, which I consider important."

After that the Marquis had not argued.

However, when they were alone, he always addressed the Major by his Christian name.

"I am in trouble," the Marquis replied in answer to his query.

The Major settled himself a little more comfortably in his chair.

"I thought when Lord Derby wanted to see you yesterday," he said quietly, "it was not entirely for the pleasure of your company!"

"No, it was not!" the Marquis replied. "It was about another investigation which he says only I can carry out."

"Where?" the Major asked briefly.

"In Morocco—Fez, to be exact."

The Major nodded his head.

"I rather suspected you would be involved in that sooner or later!"

The Marquis looked at him in surprise.

"Why on earth should you think that? What have you heard?"

"One of my friends in the Foreign Office," the Major explained, "told me a week or so ago that reports of White Slave Trafficking were becoming more frequent, and that something would have to be done about it."

He smiled before he said:

"I had the idea he was giving me that information so that I could pass it on to you."

"But you did not do so," the Marquis remarked.

"I thought you had enough on your hands for the moment!" Major Ashley replied.

The Marquis knew he was referring to Lady Hester.

There was a short silence before he said:

"That is over!"

The Major raised his eye-brows.

"So soon?"

"Not before time," the Marquis said. "To be honest, I was wondering how to escape the endless dramatics which always ensue at the 'fall of the curtain.' Then the question of going to Fez arose."

"Then what is the difficulty?" the Major asked.

The Marquis thought with a little smile of amusement that the Major knew perceptively there was more to the story than he had yet been told.

He put down his knife and fork and, pushing his plate aside, said:

"I will tell you everything, Brian, from the very beginning."

He then told him first what Lord Derby had said, but that when he left the Foreign Office, he had decided if he had to go to Fez, he had no intention of hurrying himself.

"I did not mention it to you," he said to the Major, "for the simple reason that I told Lord Derby I was enjoying myself in London—at least I thought I was."

"What occurred to spoil that enjoyment?" the Major asked.

Briefly the Marquis described Hester's behaviour with the French Ambassador the night before.

The Major knew the Marquis's obsession that any woman with whom he was involved should behave with the utmost propriety.

He had thought for some time that Lady Hester, beautiful though she undoubtedly was, lacked self-control and dignity.

The Marquis was fastidious about both.

The Major had actually been sure it was a mistake for the Marquis, of whom he was very fond, to have become embroiled with Lady Hester.

The Marquis then went on to describe how the Author at the party had urged him to visit Fez.

"It may seem to you immaterial," he said. "At the same time, I am showing you how everything began to build up to the point where I am forced to go, whether I wish to or not."

Major Ashley smiled to himself.

He had never known the Marquis to be forced into doing anything he did not want to do.

He knew better than anybody else that while the Marquis complained, he definitely enjoyed the secret missions on which he had been sent in the past.

Several of them had been terrifyingly dangerous, but the Marquis had always "turned up trumps."

It certainly relieved the monotony of passing from one beautiful woman to another, always, the Major knew, to be disillusioned.

Of course the Marquis did not think of it like that.

Because the Major was an astute judge of character, he knew the Marquis was seeking something exceptional in a woman, something that was different from the fiery affairs which burned to ashes as quickly as they were kindled.

He had a great admiration for the young man he served.

He had known when he was in the Army that the Marquis was an outstanding Officer.

The Major both admired and respected him now as his employer.

He was wondering apprehensively what he had meant by saying that he was "in trouble."

He studied the Marquis's face with his one good eye and waited for him to continue.

"I left Lady Beller's early, and as you know, her house is near here." The Marquis went on. "I decided therefore to walk home and told my coachman I would do so."

It was something he frequently did.

After a crowded party or a heavily-scented bedroom, he was in need of fresh air.

"I had almost reached the end of South Audley

Street," the Marquis went on, "when I heard a young woman shouting 'Stop thief!' "

He then related how he had met Narda.

Because he had a very retentive memory, he could repeat almost every word they had said to each other, how she had persisted, however much he argued with her, in saying she was determined to go to Fez.

"Finally, she virtually tricked me," he said, "into promising her I would let her know to-day whether I would take her with me or leave her to travel alone and meet me in Morocco."

The Marquis's voice deepened as he said:

"Of course the whole idea is ridiculous! Absolutely ridiculous! But I know, if I refuse to do as she asks, she is the type of young woman who really will try to get there on her own."

"That is impossible," the Major exclaimed, "if she is as young and pretty as you claim she is!"

"Of course it is impossible!" the Marquis agreed. "That is exactly what I said myself, but she would not listen!"

"I suppose," the Major suggested, "you could not send for her brother?"

"I thought of that," the Marquis replied. "But in the girl's own words, it would be unsporting."

The Major laughed.

"I agree with her, and so, My Lord, I see nothing for it but to take her with you in *The Dolphin*."

This was the name of the Marquis's yacht.

After the Major had spoken, the Marquis stared at him in astonishment.

"Are you seriously suggesting that I should do anything so reprehensible?" he asked. "Unless, of course, you expect me to take a party with me."

Before the Major could reply, the Marquis went on angrily:

"You know as well as I do that the one thing I dislike is a lot of idiotic women complaining because the sea is rough, and becoming suspicious because I have gone ashore without them."

The Major opened his mouth to speak, but the Marquis went on still angrily:

"It is not even as if Fez is by the sea. It is a long way inland, and I have no intention of arriving with a whole crowd of giggling sight-seers!"

"I was not suggesting that," the Major said quickly.

"Then what do you suggest?" the Marquis asked. "And how the devil would I be able to get in touch with anyone who would be of the slightest use to me if I have a lot of social idiots on my heels?"

The Marquis paused because he was almost breathless.

"I appreciate your predicament," the Major admitted, "and I realise it would be a crime to let any decent young girl travel alone across France and Spain to Morocco. Even if she survived the first two countries, she would certainly not survive the third!"

"That is exactly what I thought," the Marquis agreed, "and the only reason that she was not raped by the Sheikh, which I am sure was his intention, was that she appeared to be older than she really is. Also the necklace proved to be more desirable."

"I understand that," the Major argued, "but as the girl is so young, could she not travel with you as a relative—your sister, perhaps, or your niece?"

The Marquis stared at him.

"I expect you will not be travelling under your own name," the Major went on.

"No, of course not," the Marquis said. "I will use the passport I have as Anthony Dale, unless you can think of a better disguise."

"Fez has always been a Cultural Centre of the Moslem world," the Major remarked, "so perhaps you could pose, as you have before, as an ardent Archaeologist. As we both know, you are very knowledgeable in that field."

"I agree with that," the Marquis said. "At the same time, I do not want a tiresome young woman clinging to me."

"As a matter of fact, that might make it more convincing, and something you have not tried before," the Major replied.

"Are you really suggesting, Brian, that she could be an asset?"

"I am just thinking it out," the Major answered. "Anyone who is suspicious of you—and you know as well as I do, there are quite a number of people ready to question why you should be prying into their private affairs—would not be so alarmed if you appeared to be simply showing the Moslem World to a young and pretty relative."

The Marquis looked at him for a moment before he gave a light laugh.

"I see your reasoning, but I have no desire on my

return to be forced to behave like a gentleman because I have ruined her reputation!"

"There would be no need to do that," the Major said.

"Why not?" the Marquis enquired.

"Because she will have a chaperon on board the yacht."

"I refuse! I categorically refuse to take some tiresome, middle-aged woman with me!" the Marquis said sharply. "And if I take anyone in the same category as Hester, she would be jealous of the girl, and monopolise me in an embarrassing manner."

He paused to add:

"Besides, there is no one at the moment, as I have just told you, with whom I want to be alone on a tempestuous sea."

The Major laughed.

"I agree—that would be very tiresome!"

"Then what *are* you suggesting?" the Marquis asked in a hostile manner.

"Captain Barratt's very charming wife, with whom he is extremely happy and who spends every moment she can with him when he is ashore."

"I had no idea Barratt was married!" the Marquis exclaimed.

"He has been married for the last two years," the Major said, "and I can imagine nothing that would delight Mrs. Barratt more than to be allowed to accompany him to sea."

The Marquis was listening attentively as the Major went on:

"She would not interfere in any way with you, nor

would there be any need for you even to see her. But if the question ever arose as to your *protégée* being unchaperoned, I can assure you Mrs. Barratt is very respectable and was at one time Governess to the daughters of Lord Pershore."

"I knew, Brian, that you would have the answer!" the Marquis said. "But Heaven knows I have no wish to have this girl with me!"

"I expect, as she has told you, that she will keep out of your way," the Major said, "especially if you are in one of your disagreeable moods."

The Marquis raised his eye-brows, then he laughed.

"All right, Brian, you win!" he said. "You have found the answer to my problem. Now you had better go and 'set the wheels in motion' so that I can leave to-morrow morning."

"I will do that," the Major replied.

"The sooner this is over, the better," the Marquis added, "although, if you ask me, the whole thing is a lot of moonshine! I do not believe for one moment that large numbers of innocent white girls are being shipped to Fez to be wives of the Sheikhs, or any-one else!"

"I will collect all the information I can together with a list of contacts who we hope will be helpful," the Major said, "one man in particular who helped us when we were in Algiers, has, I know, moved to Fez."

"I know who you mean," the Marquis said, "and it is like you, Brian, to have the answer to everything."

"Not everything, unfortunately," the Major said, "and there is no need for me to warn you that you will

56

have to be extremely careful. If this traffic is really taking place, then those who are organising it are making a great deal of money. They will fight like the Devil to prevent you from interfering with them!"

He spoke very seriously, and the Marquis asked:

"Do you really believe this traffic is going on as Lord Derby seems to think? We have been sent on a 'wild-goose chase' before now!"

"I think there is definitely some such trade," the Major said slowly, "which is getting out of proportion. I understand only too well, however, that it would be a disaster if the good relations between Britain and the Sultan should be upset at the beginning of his reign."

"All right," the Marquis said heavily, "you and Lord Derby know best! I will go now and tell that tiresome child that I will pick her up to-morrow morning. I suppose *The Dolphin* is in the Thames?"

"Just below Hampton Court," the Major replied. "I will tell the Captain you will have a lady guest, and that you would be pleased if on this voyage his wife came with him. Did you say her Christian name was Narda?"

"That is right," the Marquis confirmed. "She told me it means 'joyous,' but that is not what I will be feeling at having her with me."

"You never know," the Major said. "You may find it a relief to be able to talk to somebody without looking over your shoulder, or wondering if what you have said will be repeated all over the Bazaar!"

"I doubt if Miss Warrington will be very interesting," the Marquis said with a cynical note in his voice.

"She must have the same surname as yours," the

57

Major said briskly, "so inform her that from the time she steps ashore in Morocco, her name is 'Narda Dale,' and make sure she calls you 'Uncle.' "

"I think she had better be my sister," the Marquis said. " 'Uncle' makes me feel like Methuselah!"

The Major laughed.

"All right, your sister! But for Heaven's sake, My Lord, make sure she does not fall in love with you, nor you with her!"

"There is no fear of that!" the Marquis replied. "The one thing that has always bored me is having giggling girls around me who have nothing to say for themselves."

The Major rose to his feet.

"From all you have told me, it would appear that Narda has a great deal to say for herself! Perhaps we are making a mistake in not providing her with a chaperon and a Courier and sending her overland to Fez."

"And what do I do with them once they get there?" the Marquis asked.

The Major sighed.

"That is why I thought it would be easier for her to accompany you on *The Dolphin*. And, if you are clever you might be able to persuade her to stay aboard while you make your investigations."

The Marquis groaned.

"I have an uneasy feeling," he said, "that 'come hell or high water' she will insist on coming with me wherever I go!"

"Then she is your young sister," the Major said, "enjoying the sights of Morocco with her brother, who is an expert on all the treasures it contains."

"All right, all right!" the Marquis said testily. "I see I have no alternative. But I am certain one day my kind heart and my strong sense of duty will be the death of me!"

"I doubt it," the Major replied. "You have been very successful in everything you have undertaken up until now, and I see no reason why this small adventure should be a failure."

"I only hope you are right," the Marquis remarked gloomily, "but to tell you the truth, I am apprehensive about the whole thing!"

"The alternative is to stay in London and cope with Lady Hester!"

The Marquis threw up his hands.

"I would rather face a dozen ferocious Moroccans!"

"That is exactly what you are likely to do," the Major remarked. "Now I must get busy, and I promise you, My Lord, you will be as well informed about the situation as it is possible to be in such a short time."

As he spoke, the Major went from the room without waiting for the Marquis to thank him.

As the door shut behind him, the Marquis poured himself another cup of coffee and drank it reflectively.

It had surprised him that Major Ashley had agreed that Narda should accompany him on his yacht.

Usually the Major was over-particular about his reputation, and was continually reminding him about the "spiteful tongues of the gossips."

Then he thought it over.

He realised that it was a good idea to be ostensibly visiting Fez in order to admire its architectural history.

He was very punctilious in everything that concerned his secret missions.

He would take with him a book on the Architectural Heritage of Europe written by an author named Anthony Dale.

He had paid to have it published three years ago.

'If anyone was more than just curious, he had only to say he was gathering material for his next book.

This was to be on the Architectural History of Northern Africa.

He had learnt in a hard school that to make one mistake when one was in disguise was to sign one's own death warrant.

One man of whom both he and Brian Ashley had been fond had been murdered.

Disguised as a Brahman, he had been seen to relieve nature in a European manner rather than in an Arab one.

It was easy to make such a mistake.

Two hours later he was found dead with a knife in his throat.

Fortunately Lord Derby had told him not to interfere in anything he discovered in Fez, but only to collect evidence.

That was certainly easier than having to "sail in with both fists flying."

At the same time, he had pledged himself to try to recover Narda's necklace.

'I will do my best,' he was thinking as he left the Breakfast-Room. 'But no jewel is as valuable as life.'

He thought that was something he would have to impress upon Narda.

He was not very optimistic that even if they found the Sheikh he would hand over the stolen goods.

In the hall he told the Butler as he handed him his hat that he was going for a short walk and would be back in half-an-hour.

It was a sunny morning and the air was fresh.

He walked quickly towards South Audley Street and reached the house where he had talked to Narda the previous night.

He lifted his hand preparatory to raising the well-polished silver knocker on the front door.

Before he could do so, the door was opened and Narda stood there.

"I have been watching for you," she said, "and at last you are here! I am so glad to see you!"

She looked in the daylight, he thought, lovelier than she looked the night before.

Now her face was clean of all the make-up.

She had a pink-and-white English complexion.

Her eye-lashes, blackened by mascara, had given her a hard appearance.

Now the Marquis could see they were dark at the roots and were gold at the tips, like a child's.

Her eyes were the deep blue of an alpine Gentian.

The Marquis could not help thinking that had the Sheikh seen her as she looked now he would have found her more attractive than the necklace.

She walked ahead of him into the Sitting-Room, where they had talked last night.

The sunshine was coming through the windows.

The Marquis saw there were several vases of flowers arranged around the room.

Their fragrance permeated the air.

She shut the door after he had passed through it and looked up at him questioningly.

He knew she was apprehensive that once again he would refuse to take her with him.

He was, however, still so annoyed with her that he did not speak.

Instead, he stood with his back to the mantelpiece, below which there was a small fire burning in the fireplace.

At last Narda ran towards him to ask:

"What have . . . you . . . decided? I have not been . . . able to . . . sleep because I was so . . . worried you . . . would make me . . . go to Fez . . . alone."

"Are you still determined to do anything so extremely foolish?" the Marquis asked.

She nodded.

Then she said in a very small voice:

"I . . . I would much rather . . . go with . . . you."

"Then I suppose I shall have to let you," the Marquis said. "But . . . "

Before he could finish the sentence, she gave a cry which seemed to echo round the walls.

"You agree? You . . . agree? Oh . . . how . . . wonderful! I knew you were too much of a . . . sportsman to leave . . . me to . . . my fate!"

"I am not going to do that," the Marquis said, "and I will take you with me in my yacht—but only on one condition."

"What is . . . that?"

"That you will do exactly as I tell you without making any protests if I consider it is the right thing for you to do."

"I promise . . . of course I promise!" she cried. "But if it is . . . something impossible . . . then you must . . . be generous enough not to . . . suggest it."

The Marquis laughed because he could not help it.

"You are attempting to wriggle out of giving me the answer I want," he said. "Yes—or no?"

"Yes!"

"I shall keep you to that," he asserted.

"When are we leaving? Please say 'at once,' just in case something . . . stops us."

"I will pick you up to-morrow morning at ten o'clock," he said.

She gave another cry of joy.

He thought for one moment she was going to fling herself into his arms.

"Now, just remember," he said, "we are going to Fez because we want to retrieve the necklace which means so much to you."

He paused for a moment before he said:

"I have been thinking it over, and it might be a mistake for me to arrive as the Marquis of Calvadale, and for you to be Miss Warrington."

He realised that Narda was staring at him in surprise, and he explained:

"If the Sheikh learns that you are in Fez with an English nobleman, he might easily just disappear into the desert, where it would be quite impossible for us to find him."

"Yes . . . of course! That is very . . . clever

of . . . you," Narda agreed breathlessly.

"Also," the Marquis continued, "it could easily cause a great deal of trouble if you travel with me without a chaperon."

"Do we have to take some tiresome old woman with us?" Narda asked. "She would definitely . . . disapprove of me."

"I am sure she would!" the Marquis remarked sternly. "And that is why I have made arrangements to which I think you will agree."

Narda looked at him nervously and he said:

"First of all, you will be my young sister to whom I am showing the beauties of Fez. I will tell you your surname later, which will be the same as mine."

"I am to go in disguise! Narda exclaimed. "How . . . exciting! I shall . . . enjoy . . . that!"

"Being in disguise is not a joke," the Marquis cautioned. "It can sometimes prove disastrous, for if people discover they are being deceived, they often feel insulted."

"I think I can understand that," Narda said, "and I will be very careful not to say or do anything which would make the people we meet suspicious."

"That is no more than I expect," the Marquis said gravely.

He saw the excitement in Narda's blue eyes. He knew it appealed to her imagination in the same way that she had enjoyed pretending to be a "Gaiety Girl."

"Lastly," he said, "I am arranging for the wife of the ship's Captain to be aboard on this voyage. She will, of course, not interfere with us in any way. At the same time, should there later be any questions asked regarding the propriety of your travelling with me, you have been properly chaperoned."

Narda clasped her hands together.

"That is clever . . . very clever," she exclaimed. "I might have known when I first saw you that you would be brilliant at anything you undertook! Just as your horses always win on the race-course, we shall win the battle of Fez!"

"It is a mistake to be too optimistic," the Marquis warned her. "I consider it a definite possibility that we might fail."

"While I am quite . . . quite . . . certain that with you . . . I will . . . succeed!" Narda retorted.

chapter four

THE next morning the Marquis again sent for Major Ashley while he was having breakfast.

"Good-morning, My Lord!" the Major said as he came into the room. "Everything is arranged and *The Dolphin* will be ready as soon as you arrive."

"What I am going to do now," the Marquis said in a cold, determined voice, "is to go and see Lord Derby and tell him that I am leaving, and that I also require some money."

"I was going to remind you of that," the Major said hastily.

"In the meantime," the Marquis went on as if he had not spoken, "I want you to pick up Miss Warrington and take her to *The Dolphin*, and while you are about it, tell her to behave herself, or I will throw her overboard!"

The Major laughed.

"I would hardly expect you to do that, My Lord, but

I will certainly warn her to avoid any confrontations with her host."

"I cannot imagine why I got myself into this mess!" the Marquis exclaimed angrily.

He pushed aside his plate and left the room.

His carriage was waiting outside, and he got in it and drove away without saying anymore.

Major Ashley, however, had made all the arrangements, and the Marquis's valet left a few minutes afterwards with the luggage.

There was no hurry, for the Major realised the Marquis would be some time with Lord Derby.

In fact, he arrived at Warrington House in South Audley Street soon after half-past nine.

Narda was waiting and had been asking herself for the last twenty-four hours what she would do in the event that the Marquis refused to take her.

It would mean that she would have to travel alone to Fez or else confess the truth to her brother about the necklace and endure his fury.

She told herself bitterly that she would never trust a man again.

It had never struck her that anyone who moved in the Social World, even if it was the type of party she had attended the previous night, would stoop to be what was nothing more than a common thief, least of all a man of the Sheikh's importance.

She noticed he had been treated with respect by the male members of the party.

"How can this have happened?" she asked herself over and over again during the night when she could not sleep.

She had risen soon after dawn.

Without calling a maid, she packed everything she thought she would require either for the sea voyage or if she had to travel overland.

She was not certain exactly what she would need.

She only hoped when she finished that the Marquis would not be annoyed at her having so much luggage.

She had finished breakfast, finding it almost impossible to swallow anything, when she heard a carriage draw up outside.

She ran to the window.

A footman was jumping down to open the carriage door.

With a leap of her heart she thought she had won and the Marquis was taking her with him to Morocco.

Then she saw that it was not the Marquis who stepped out from the carriage, but an older man who was a stranger.

It was with the greatest constraint that she did not run out into the hall to ask him who he was.

Instead, she waited for the elderly maid, who never hurried herself, to open the front door.

Then the visitor was brought into the Sitting-Room.

"Major Ashley to see you, Miss Narda!" the maid announced.

As Narda looked up enquiringly, she realised that the man coming into the room had a black patch on one eye.

He was, however, good-looking, but older than the Marquis.

"Good-morning, Miss Warrington," he said. "I

know you were expecting His Lordship, but he has an important appointment and sent me in his place. I am His Lordship's Secretary."

"Have you . . . come to . . . tell me that he is . . . refusing to take me with him to Fez?" Narda asked.

Major Ashley smiled.

"On the contrary, I am to take you to his yacht which is moored on the Thames just below Hampton Court."

Narda's eyes lit up, and she made a sound that was one of joy.

"I am to . . . go with . . . him? But this is . . . wonderful!" she exclaimed. "I was so afraid he would make me go overland, and I was not certain whether I could . . . manage it on . . . my own."

"Of course you could not," the Major said. "It would be impossible for anyone as young as yourself to travel all that way alone."

"But there is no one to go with me," Narda said simply, "and I expect you already know the reason why I must go to Fez."

"As His Lordship's Private Secretary, he often takes me into his confidence," the Major admitted. "But I promise you, Miss Warrington, nobody else is aware of the predicament you are in."

"That is the right word for it!" Narda said dismally. "It is a terrible predicament, and my brother will be very, very angry if I do not get back the necklace."

"I cannot imagine how you will be able to do so," Major Ashley said, "but you could have no one better to help you than His Lordship."

Narda did not answer for a moment.

Then she said in a small voice:

"I . . . I am afraid he is not very . . . pleased at the idea."

"I will talk to you about that as we drive to *The Dolphin*," the Major said. "Are your things packed?"

"Yes, of course," Narda replied quickly. "I have only to put on my hat and coat."

The Major had in fact noticed the pile of trunks in the hall as he entered the house.

Miss Warrington clearly intended to make herself attractive on the voyage.

He remembered that it was his job to inform her that she was to be as unobtrusive as possible, and it was not going to be easy.

As Narda ran from the room, he thought how very pretty she was, and how gracefully she moved.

Perhaps, after all, the Marquis would not find the journey as tedious and as boring as he had expected it to be.

Then Major Ashley compared Narda in his mind with the sophisticated women like Lady Hester with whom the Marquis always amused himself.

He knew the only thing that would please His Lordship would be to see as little of Miss Warrington as possible.

It was obvious the Marquis had no use for very young girls.

In fact, the Major doubted if he had ever talked with a *débutante*, let alone condescended to dance with one.

"I will do my best," he told himself, "but I expect that by the end of the voyage the wretched girl will have been snubbed into silence, and if she is unhappy about it, it will be her own fault!"

He went into the hall and, going to the front-door, told the footman to put Narda's luggage on the back of the carriage.

He had brought a travelling carriage which was made especially to carry luggage.

But two of her bags and her dressing-case had to be placed inside the carriage on the seat with its back to the horses.

Sooner than he expected, Narda came downstairs wearing an attractive little hat which haloed her fair hair.

She was carrying over her arm a fur-lined cloak.

The Major thought it a wise precaution against the cold winds she might encounter in the Bay of Biscay.

"I am ready," she announced, "but I am afraid I have very little money with me. I suppose I should have gone to the Bank."

"You will not have to pay for your journey to Morocco," the Major replied, "and I am sure if you require anything while you are there, His Lordship will be able to cash a cheque for you."

"I hoped you would say that," Narda replied, "but it is embarrassing to impose on His Lordship, and he might resent it."

The Major thought it was just one more item to increase the resentment building up in the Marquis at having to take her with him.

Aloud he said:

"If you are ready, I think we should go. That will give you plenty of time to unpack before the yacht reaches the open sea."

"If you are suggesting that I shall be sea-sick," Narda replied, "I can tell you that I am a very good sailor!"

As she spoke, she walked down the steps to the carriage.

The Major followed her, and as the carriage drove away Narda said:

"I hope Aunt Edith was not listening to what I have just said."

"Why is that?" the Major enquired.

"Because I left a note for her saying that I am going to stay with friends in the country and of course did not mention that I was going abroad."

"We must hope she is not curious enough to ask too many questions!" the Major said, feeling this was a minor detail.

"My brother will not be back for two or three weeks," Narda went on, "so there will be no one to worry about me, unless, of course, Aunt Edith writes to him, which is unlikely."

"That, at any rate, is satisfactory," the Major replied. "Now I want to talk to you about the voyage."

There was a serious note in his voice which made Narda give him a sharp glance.

"I know what you are going to say," she said, "that the Marquis is furious at my forcing myself upon him, and it would therefore be wise to keep out of his way as much as possible."

The Major stared at her in surprise.

He had never met a woman who wished to keep out of the Marquis's way.

Indeed, most women seemed determined to make him notice them by whatever means they could.

"How did you know that was what I was going to say?" he asked.

"I was reading your thoughts," Narda replied. "It was not very difficult, considering how angry His Lordship was when I insisted on accompanying him."

The Major did not reply, and she went on:

"You must see that I *have* to do so! How, even if he saw it, could he recognise the necklace? Moreover, he has never seen the Sheikh."

"If you ask me," the Major answered, "I think it will prove easier to find the Sheikh than to find the necklace."

"I *have* to try to get it back," Narda insisted, "and besides, it was a very dirty trick he played on me when he drugged me and disappeared."

"I agree with you," the Major replied. "But, of course, as His Lordship told me, you should not have been at the party in the first place."

"I know that," Narda agreed ruefully, "and it was very wrong of me. But that makes it all the more important for me to get back my brother's necklace. You must realise that I cannot simply sit tamely at home and admit it has gone."

The Major began to feel some sympathy for her.

At the same time, he could not forget the Marquis's instructions.

"What I advise you to do," he said, "is to leave everything in His Lordship's capable hands. He is very experienced at judging people's characters, and also has an unusual knowledge of the Arab World."

The Major was choosing his words carefully, but Narda said impetuously:

"I feel sure that His Lordship, as he has travelled so extensively, has been involved in strange and dangerous situations before."

The Major looked at her in astonishment.

"Why should you think that?" he asked.

"I do not know," Narda replied. "I just felt it about him. I knew when he said he would help me if he could that it was not just an idle promise such as an ordinary man might have made."

The Major thought she was extremely perceptive, or else she had heard some gossip about what he had always believed was a very well-kept secret.

Since he himself had become involved, the Major had always been prepared for questions about the Marquis's secret activities.

But he had found, and it did not surprise him, that all anyone wanted to talk about was His Lordship's love-affairs.

The women who pursued the Marquis had usually confided in Major Ashley.

They had made it quite clear to him what they wanted.

This certainly did not in any way involve the sort of situation to which Narda was referring.

"All you have to do," he said aloud, "is to assist His Lordship if ever he asks you to do so, but otherwise to rely on his very able brain."

Narda laughed.

"What you are really saying is that I should keep out of His Lordship's way," she said, "and behave as if I were half-witted!"

"I did not say that!" the Major objected.

"But you *thought* it!" she persisted.

They drove for a little while in silence.

Then Narda said:

"I will try to do as you have told me. At the same time, when we get there I must find the Sheikh and the necklace."

"I am sure it would be wiser to leave everything to His Lordship," the Major said painstakingly.

"I will remember what you have said," Narda replied, "but I am making no promises. I have to think of my problem and get back the necklace before my brother becomes aware that it has gone."

"Then all I can do," the Major replied with a sigh, "is to wish you *Bon Voyage* and the very best luck! But you will not help your cause if you annoy His Lordship!"

Narda gave him a sideways glance, and he saw that she was smiling.

He was aware that she knew exactly why he had said what he had, that he had been given instructions to do so.

'She is certainly more intelligent than most girls of her age!' he thought.

They reached the yacht.

As the horses came to a standstill, the Major felt apprehensively that he had failed to impress upon her what her behaviour should be on the voyage to Morocco and, even more important, after they got there.

* * *

The Marquis arrived at the Foreign Office and asked to see Lord Derby.

A few minutes later, when he walked into his office, the Secretary of State for Foreign Affairs stared at him in astonishment.

"I did not expect to see you so soon, or so early, Favian!" he exclaimed.

"I know that," the Marquis replied, "but I am in fact leaving for Fez immediately."

"You take my breath away!" Lord Derby exclaimed. "What can have happened to precipitate such a decision?"

"Something I do not intend to tell you," the Marquis said. "What I want, My Lord, is money and my passport as Anthony Dale."

The passport, because it was so secret, was always kept at the Foreign Office.

This ensured that no inquisitive servant or guest should see it in the Marquis's house.

Without saying anything, Lord Derby rang a bell and one of his Senior Officials answered it.

"I want the passport, Jackson, which is in the name of Anthony Dale," Lord Derby said, "and also some French and Moroccan money."

"Which looks well used," the Marquis added.

The Official withdrew and Lord Derby said:

"I am extremely grateful, Favian, that you are taking this seriously. As it happens, I received a report only yesterday which confirms what I have already told you."

"I will try to find out all you want to know," the Marquis promised, "and I want you to tell me anything you know about a Sheikh Rachid Shriff, who has recently been in London."

This involved consultation with another Official.

He was away for about twenty minutes before he returned to report that Sheikh Rachid Shriff had been in London recently, had been a visitor six months ago, and also the year before.

He had given a number of large and expensive parties and associated with some of the most important people, as well as with some questionable men who were suspected of dealing in drugs.

"I am afraid, My Lord," the Official who brought the news said apologetically, "there is not a great deal known about this Sheikh, except that he has great success with the ladies!"

"That applies to a great number of people!" Lord Derby replied.

When they were alone, he said to the Marquis:

"Is that of any help?"

"It is what I suspected," the Marquis said, "and I do not suppose I shall have much difficulty in finding him!"

"I gather you do not intend to tell me why you are interested in him," Lord Derby remarked. "But if you are in trouble, you know where you can always find help."

"Yes, I know that," the Marquis replied. "But I hope I shall not be away for long, and can bring you back the information you require."

"I need not tell you how grateful I am, Favian," Lord Derby said. "I would not have asked you to do this had it not been of great political importance."

The Marquis laughed.

"Are your requests ever anything else?" he asked.

The Official who had been sent to find the passport brought it in.

It was worded in the usual manner in elegant copper-plate writing and signed by Lord Derby.

The Marquis read it, then he said:

"I want added to it the name of Narda Dale, sister of Anthony."

For a moment Lord Derby stared at him in astonishment.

Then he asked:

"Sister?"

"Sister!" the Marquis replied.

Lord Derby gave the order and the Official went away again.

As the door closed behind him, Lord Derby asked:

"Now, what is all this about? I have never known you to travel with a 'sister' before!"

"She is a tiresome young girl whom I have promised to assist by retrieving from the Sheikh something he has stolen from her," the Marquis replied.

He spoke reluctantly, as if he disliked explanations, and Lord Derby said:

"Well, I suppose you know what you are doing. But I have never known you in the past to take a woman with you when you are on business, which is a polite word for it."

"I know, I know!" the Marquis agreed testily. "But this is something I cannot avoid, and in fact, if you think it over, it provides me with a disguise which will be more convincing than it might otherwise be."

"There is some logic in that," Lord Derby said. "But she might also be indiscreet, and that could be a disaster as far as you are concerned."

The Marquis did not speak, and Lord Derby went on:

"You have always surprised and delighted me with the success of the missions you have undertaken in the past, Favian, and no one ever suspected for a moment that you were anything but a carefree bachelor seeking out the prettiest women available."

The Marquis laughed.

"Well, it is true," Lord Derby said, "and it terrifies me to think that on this occasion you are taking some chattering creature with you who will tell her best friend that you travel incognito and her best friend will undoubtedly tell the world!"

"You must leave that to me," the Marquis said in a harsh voice. "I will make quite certain that she knows as little as possible and keeps her mouth shut!"

"Better men than you have been destroyed by a woman who talks too much," Lord Derby remarked darkly.

"All women do that," the Marquis replied. "I assure you, however, I will make certain this one does nothing of the sort."

Lord Derby metaphorically shrugged his shoulders.

There was nothing he could do.

He was thinking that for the first time the Marquis

was taking a step in the dark which he might later regret bitterly.

* * *

When an hour later the Marquis drove away from the Foreign Office, he was thinking the same thing.

"Why the hell did I ever say I would help the girl?" he asked himself. "If I had walked on, telling her it was none of my business, I would not now be risking something which is important for the sake of a necklace!"

The whole idea of it made him scowl.

At the same time, he knew it would have been impossible for him to deliberately "wash his hands" of the situation.

If he had done so, Narda would have gone overland alone to Morocco.

If what he had anticipated happened, he knew it would be on his conscience for the rest of his life.

"It is not my business," he nevertheless told himself. "How could I have been such a quixotic fool when I have a job to do which is of real importance?"

But he could not help feeling that if he could persuade Narda to behave as he wished, she might prove an asset rather than an encumbrance.

If things were as difficult as Lord Derby suspected, then even an Archaeologist asking questions and wandering about alone might arouse comment.

On the other hand, if he was pointing out the sights to his young sister, he could just be a tourist of no particular importance to anybody.

The Marquis was well aware, however, as he drove on, that Lord Derby had put his finger on the weak spot—a woman's tongue.

"I will somehow make certain she does not talk," the Marquis swore to himself, "even if I have to throttle her to make her obey me!"

* * *

As Narda stepped aboard *The Dolphin* she thought it was the most beautiful yacht she had ever seen.

She was also sure it was much the fastest.

Major Ashley introduced her to the Captain before taking her on a tour of the ship.

It was in fact a comparatively new acquisition of the Marquis's.

He had considered his old yacht too slow, especially if he was being pursued by other ships.

Every new device had been incorporated in the building of *The Dolphin*.

The engine and a great number of gadgets were more advanced than on any other vessel afloat.

The Dolphin was also very attractively decorated.

Narda was thrilled with her cabin, which had a pink carpet and pink curtains over the port-holes.

The white walls, fitted with white cupboards and drawers, gave the cabin the impression of being larger than it actually was.

As the Marquis was not yet aboard, Major Ashley allowed her to peep into the Master Cabin.

It was naturally the largest in the yacht and filled the whole of the stern.

It was more severely decorated than the other cabins and certainly more masculine in appearance.

At the same time, it had a magnificence about it which Narda thought was very appropriate.

Then she discovered something which thrilled her more than anything else.

In the Saloon as well as in the Marquis's private study there was a large number of books.

She saw at a glance that many of them were about foreign countries and guessed there would be some about Morocco.

She told the Major what she was seeking, and he said:

"Because I knew where His Lordship was heading, I included in his luggage nearly a dozen books on Morocco, so you will have plenty to read before you arrive."

"What you are saying is that if I am reading I shall not be disturbing His Lordship!" Narda said.

Her eyes were twinkling.

"Now I must concede that you *can* read my thoughts!" Major Ashley remarked.

They both laughed.

Then, as Narda's trunks were brought into her cabin, she said:

"Perhaps I had better unpack."

"That is a good idea," the Major agreed, "and I will let you know when His Lordship arrives."

He saw by the expression in Narda's eyes that she was amused.

She guessed that he was feeling anxious about his employer's reactions.

"You can tell him I shall be very amenable," she said, "so long as he does what I want once we reach our destination."

"I will tell him nothing of the sort!" the Major replied quickly. "You must fight your own battle, if that is what you intend to do, and my only suggestion is that since neither of you can escape, you try to make the voyage as peaceful and interesting as possible."

He thought as he spoke that would be an impossibility as far as the Marquis was concerned.

However, he had to admit that Narda was not in the least what he had expected.

Knowing how young she was, he had thought she would be either shy and retiring, or else nervously gushing and somewhat gauche.

But she was none of those things.

She had a sense of humour and at the same time a poise which he might have expected to find only in a much older woman.

"I think His Lordship may be in for a surprise!" he told himself as he walked up the companionway, leaving Narda in her cabin.

* * *

Narda had found room for her gowns in the cupboards, and had almost emptied her trunks when there was a knock on the door.

She opened it and saw standing outside a wiry little man whom she guessed was the Marquis's valet.

"Ow, ye've done yer unpackin', Miss!" he exclaimed. "There wasn't no need. I'd 'ave done it for yer."

"It is very kind of you," Narda replied, "but I expect you had plenty to do for His Lordship."

"Everythin's spick an' span," the valet replied. "My name's Yates, an' I only come to say if there's anythin' I can do for ye, Miss, it'll be a pleasure!"

"Thank you," Narda answered. "What I would like, if it is possible for you to get them, is the books on Morocco which I understand were packed in His Lordship's luggage. I would like to read them on the voyage."

"That's easy!" Yates answered. "I've already put 'em in 'is Lordship's study."

He disappeared into the Master Cabin and returned with his arms full of books.

"Take yer pick, Miss," he said, "an' I'll change 'em as soon as ye've finished one."

Narda smiled at him and said:

"I am very, very grateful."

She looked over the books before choosing three.

"I will start with these," she said.

"If yer finishes 'em too quick, Miss, I'll be sure ye're skippin' a few pages!" Yates remarked.

"I read very quickly," Narda replied, "and I shall skip nothing in these because I am very interested in Morocco."

The valet gave her a searching glance.

She knew he was thinking that most women he knew were more interested in his master than in anything they could find in a book.

As Yates returned to his Master's cabin, Narda shut

her door and gave a little laugh.

"The trouble with the Marquis," she told herself, "is that he is too puffed up with his own importance. If he thinks I am more interested in him than in Morocco, he is going to find he is mistaken!"

She put the books down by her bed and thought with delight of all the others there were aboard.

She had been so much alone in the country while her father was ill.

But she had found that reading was an antidote to loneliness and boredom.

Fortunately, because her father was a very intelligent man, he had a large Library.

He would discuss with her what she was reading.

He would add to her knowledge with stories of his own experiences and anecdotes which made everything come to life.

It was almost as if she had travelled to the places herself.

She had always been interested in North Africa.

She had never dreamed she would be so lucky as to visit Morocco.

Her brother had no wish to travel.

He was content to live in England and enjoy his racing and to spend his time when he was in London with friends.

Sometimes he went to the sort of parties to which he made it quite clear he could never take her.

He read only the sporting columns of the newspapers on the back pages.

Narda, however, read the political news and anything that appertained to other countries in the world.

Especially those she had read about and discussed with her father.

She opened one of the books now which she had taken from Yates and started to scan the first page.

Then as she heard a commotion above her head she knew that the Marquis had arrived.

She wondered what he was saying to Major Ashley.

She guessed the latter would repeat the conversation they had had in the carriage.

'His Lordship will want to know that his orders have been carried out,' she thought, 'and that I have been told to keep out of his way!'

She sat down in an armchair and went on reading the first pages of the book.

She could hear people moving about on the deck.

"His Lordship need not worry on my account," she told herself. "I shall be quite content to be on my own until we reach Morocco. Then I will have to make him find the Sheikh, and help me get back the necklace."

She smiled.

"I am quite certain, until that time, I shall find his books much more absorbing than he is!"

chapter five

THE sea was calmer in the Bay of Biscay than the Marquis had expected.

He suddenly realised that he had not seen Narda for the three days since he came on board.

When she did not appear at luncheon on the first day, he thought she was preparing herself for the sea.

It became "choppy" when the yacht reached the end of the Thames Estuary.

Turning into the Strait of Dover, *The Dolphin* began to pitch and toss.

He thought that, like most women, Narda would be feeling seasick and had therefore been sensible enough to stay in her cabin.

He thought the same thing as they passed down the English Channel with the wind whipping up the waves.

When *The Dolphin* entered the Bay of Biscay, the Marquis was quite certain Narda would not set foot on deck.

However, he thought he had been remiss in not enquiring as to her well-being.

He was still feeling furious at her intrusion, although so far she had been no trouble.

Therefore, when he was dressing, he said to Yates:

"I suppose Miss Warrington is all right and has not been too overcome by sea-sickness?"

Yates grinned.

"She ain't bin seasick, M'Lord," he said, "she's bin readin' an' 'as gone through seven of yer Lordship's books about Morocco an' asked me for three more."

The Marquis stared at his valet.

"Reading?"

"That's right, M'Lord."

"And—she has not been sea-sick?"

"Not 'er, M'Lord!"

"Then why has she kept to her cabin?"

Yates hesitated.

The Marquis knew he did not wish to say that Narda was avoiding him.

Then after a moment Yates informed him:

"She goes up on deck when ye've retired, M'Lord, and again at dawn. Otherwise she says she's never enjoyed herself more!"

The Marquis was astounded.

He had never imagined that any woman, young or old, would deliberately avoid him and prefer a book to his company.

Having finished his breakfast, he went as usual onto the bridge.

It was where he liked to spend most of his time when he was aboard, as he enjoyed navigating his own ship.

This morning, however, his mind was on Narda reading in her cabin.

He wondered if he should send for her.

He was still doubtful that it would be a wise thing to do when he was told luncheon was ready.

When he had finished what was an excellent meal, as good as anything he ate at home, he said to the Chief Steward:

"Ask Miss Warrington if she will dine with me this evening. I suggest we do so at seven-thirty."

The Steward hurried away to obey his order.

The Marquis was aware by the expression in the man's eyes that he thought it strange that up to now Miss Warrington had not emerged from her cabin.

He waited until the Steward returned.

"Miss Warrington thanks, M'Lord, for th' invitation," he said, "and'll be delighted to dine with Your Lordship at seven-thirty."

The Marquis went out on deck.

He wondered if he was making a mistake.

After all, Narda had kept out of his way, which was what he had wanted.

Perhaps it was advisable to see as little as possible of her before they arrived in Morocco.

Yet he knew he had to instruct her as to how she should behave as his "sister."

He thought it would be difficult to be convincing if they had not spoken to each other previously.

* * *

Narda was amused by the Marquis's invitation.

She had wondered when the moment would come when he felt he must talk to her, however much he resented her being aboard.

'He can hardly accuse me of having been a nuisance!' she thought.

She spent the afternoon enjoying a book which described the different tribes that lived in Morocco.

She was most interested in the Berbers.

However, she was fascinated also by the Almoravids, who were the descendants of the Berbers who had conquered the Sahara.

They had carried Islam to the frontiers of Black Africa.

It was in Morocco that Berber Islam reached its zenith.

The Marinids, who had settled in Eastern Morocco, succeeded in wresting the country little by little from the other tribes.

They had made Fez their capital.

There was so much to read about Fez, and Narda was intrigued by the various names it had been called over the years.

Fez el-Bali, or Fez the Old, had been founded by A.D. 800.

Fez the Holy was one of the most revered religious centres of the Moslem world.

There was also Fez Imperial and Fez the Secret—a city of political intrigue.

The more she read, the more she realised that even apart from the Sheikh and her necklace she longed to see Fez.

When she dressed for dinner she put on one of the prettiest gowns that she had bought when she first came to London.

She had thought that her brother would take her to a number of smart social parties.

As he had not done so, the dress had remained forlornly in her wardrobe.

She hoped now, although she thought it very unlikely, the Marquis would appreciate the one she was wearing.

In fact, when she came into the Saloon where he was waiting, he was astonished by her beauty.

He had thought that first night that even with her gaudy make-up she was very lovely.

Now, in the clear evening light coming into the Saloon, she seemed like a being from another world.

She stood just inside the door, looking at him, not nervously, as he might have expected, but questioningly, as if she were waiting for him to explain himself.

"Good-evening, Narda!" he said. "I must apologise for not having invited you before, but it was only today that I learned you were not stricken, as I had supposed, with sea-sickness."

"I was carrying out your orders, My Lord, to be unobtrusive," Narda replied.

She did not say it resentfully, but spoke as if the idea amused her.

She walked gracefully towards him, apparently unaware that the ship was rolling slightly.

She sat down in one of the comfortable chairs which were fixed to the floor.

"Would you like a glass of champagne?" the Marquis asked.

"Thank you," Narda replied.

He put the glass in her hand, saying as he did so:

"I hope they have been looking after you and you have had everything you require?"

"Your valet has been very helpful," she replied, "and I must congratulate you on your Library, from which I have learned a great many things I wanted to know."

"I am afraid it contains little in the way of novels," the Marquis said.

"I cannot imagine any novel being more exciting than the books I have read about Morocco and especially, of course, Fez!" Narda answered.

The Marquis wondered if she was trying to impress him.

However, as they sat down to dinner, he found she had acquired a great deal of knowledge about Moroccan history, almost as much, if not more, than he knew himself.

"Why are you so interested," he asked, "apart from the fact that you are searching for the Sheikh?"

"I have always wanted to go to Morocco," Narda explained. "I went to Constantinople with Papa and Mama about five years ago, and we also visited Cairo, but I have always thought North Africa had a charm that was all its own."

The Marquis was surprised.

"Why did your father take you to Constantinople?" he enquired.

"Of course, you are not aware that Papa was at one time in the Diplomatic Service," Narda explained. "He retired when he came into the title and estate, which he had to look after, and which is quite large."

The Marquis was listening as she went on:

"I suppose, as Papa had travelled around the world, it made me want to do the same. But though I was unable to visit a great number of places physically, I was able to do so mentally by reading about them."

Now the Marquis was definitely astonished.

He had never met a woman before who had troubled when she went abroad to read the history of the country she was in.

Even if she went to Paris or Rome she certainly would not be interested in any country she could not visit personally.

During a very good dinner he found himself telling Narda about the places to which he had been.

He added to her knowledge in the same way that in the past her father had helped her.

The Stewards removed the dishes that contained fruit.

The Marquis rose and moved towards the comfortable chairs at the other end of the Saloon.

Narda, however, left the table, and instead of following him, she walked towards the door.

As she reached it, she turned back to say:

"Thank you, My Lord, for an extremely interesting and exciting dinner. Good-night!"

The Marquis looked at her incredulously.

Before he could say "Wait!" she had gone, and he thought it would be undignified to run after her.

He could hardly believe she had returned to her cabin and no longer wished to talk to him.

Any other woman would have wanted to stay until the early hours of the morning.

When he thought it over, he knew that was not the whole story.

Any other woman would have been flirting with him and enticing him.

She would have been trying with every wile and trick in her repertoire to lure him into making love to her.

But this innocent young girl, while she appreciated his experience and his knowledge, was obviously not aware of him as an attractive man.

It was a situation the Marquis had never encountered before.

When later he went up on deck, he wondered if Narda thought him too old to be anything but an encyclopaedia.

However much he tried to avoid it, he found himself still thinking of her when he went to bed.

He found it difficult to sleep.

Suddenly he remembered Yates telling him that she went out on deck very early in the morning, then late at night after he had retired to bed.

Because he could hardly believe this was true, he looked at his clock.

It was nearly one o'clock in the morning.

"Yates is talking nonsense!" he told himself.

Nevertheless, he was curious and could not resist getting out of bed.

He put on the long, warm robe which he wore when he was aboard *The Dolphin*.

It was made of a heavy wool lined with silk.

It was also frogged, so that it gave him a military appearance.

He put on a pair of soft shoes.

Opening his cabin door, he found as he expected that the corridor was lit by a single light.

He went to the companionway, telling himself as he went up it that he was being absurd.

Of course Narda was asleep, and the sooner he went back to bed the better.

All the same, he went out on deck.

The sea was calm and *The Dolphin* was moving at a slightly slower speed than in the daytime.

Overhead the sky was brilliant with stars.

The moon revealed in the distance the dark outline of the Spanish coast.

The deck looked deserted, and the Marquis was just about to return to his cabin.

Then he saw a slight figure at the far end of the deck.

He walked towards her and realised that Narda was leaning over the rail.

She was wearing a fur-lined cloak over what he thought was a nightgown and perhaps a *négligée*.

Her fair hair was falling over her shoulders.

As he came up to stand beside her, she did not turn to look at him but continued to gaze out to sea.

He realised she was looking at the phosphorus on

the water which changed shape with the slight movements of the surface.

He stood beside her in silence until she said:

"On a night like this I feel sure I will see a mermaid, or perhaps they find these waters too cold for them."

There was a dreamy quality about her voice.

It was as if she were expressing her thoughts rather than speaking to him.

"The first time I went in a yacht when I was a very little boy," the Marquis replied, "I was quite certain that I saw a mermaid. My father told me it was a porpoise, but I did not believe him."

"I am sure he was wrong and you did see a mermaid!" Narda replied. "The ancient mariners often saw mermaids, and they cannot all have been mistaken."

"Of course not," the Marquis agreed.

"I suppose you call your yacht *The Dolphin* because it has a special place in mythology, especially as Apollo rode on one."

The Marquis smiled.

"I was not actually thinking of myself as Apollo!"

"Of course not!" Narda replied.

He felt she spoke a little too fervently for it to be complimentary.

But she went on:

"At the same time, while he brought light and hope to the world, you in your own way, if secretly, do the same."

The Marquis looked at her sharply.

"Why should you think that?" he enquired.

For a moment she did not reply.

Then she said:

"I think you are going to Fez for some very important reason and, although it may be dangerous, I am quite sure you will achieve your objective."

The Marquis was stunned.

"I cannot imagine why you should think that!" he said after a moment.

Narda did not reply.

But he knew she was smiling as she continued to look into the waves in search of a mermaid.

*　　*　　*

The following day at the Marquis's insistence they had both luncheon and dinner together.

He found, however, that between the two meals she managed to disappear from his sight.

Major Ashley had obviously made it clear she was not to bore him with her company.

At the same time, he told himself a little ruefully that it was good for his ego.

Perhaps he was not quite as attractive as he had believed himself to be.

He could imagine no other woman he knew deliberately limiting her time with him to two meals a day while they were alone together on the same yacht.

It was only when they were drawing nearer to their destination that the Marquis said:

"Do not leave me, Narda. I want to talk to you."

He spoke before she had risen from the table.

She therefore walked, as he did, and sat down in

one of the comfortable chairs.

When the Stewards had left the Saloon the Marquis began:

"You will understand that it would be a great mistake for us to arrive in Morocco as ourselves."

Narda nodded.

"I thought you would say that."

"I have therefore," the Marquis went on, "had a passport made out in the name of Anthony Dale, an Archaeologist, and his sister Narda Dale, who accompanies him."

Narda laughed.

"I suppose, My Lord," she said, "I should feel highly honoured to be allowed to be your 'sister,' knowing how much you resent my being with you."

"I am not resenting it now," the Marquis replied. "I realise, Narda, and this is the truth, that you are a very intelligent young woman, and I have greatly enjoyed the conversations we have had at mealtimes."

He thought as he spoke that that was definitely the truth.

He felt when he had talked to Narda more as if he were talking to one of his men-friends.

It was even as if she were Brian Ashley.

He realised that her knowledge of the customs of other lands would have been extraordinary if she had been a man.

When she told him remarkable facts about them, he realised that she knew even more about them than he did himself.

But never by a word or a look had she in any way treated him as if he were exciting as a man.

"After what you have said to me," the Marquis went on, "I think you realise that it is absolutely essential that no one should guess for one instant that we are incognito."

Narda nodded and he continued:

"One careless remark could prove fatal! You must therefore be on your guard from the moment you set foot in Morocco until we are back on *The Dolphin*."

This was what Narda had expected, and she answered:

"If you will tell me what you want me to do, I promise you I will be very careful to obey you."

"Thank you," the Marquis said. "Now let me explain who I am and why we are visiting Morocco."

He showed her the book he had published on Architecture.

He would appear to be showing her Fez because of its great historical interest.

He also told her that he would make all the enquiries about the Sheikh.

She was not to make any investigations herself, or appear to be curious about anything but the places he showed her and, of course, the history of Fez.

"That will be easy," Narda said, "as I already know so much about it."

"The people with whom we will be associating, and of course our guides, will expect you to be ignorant," the Marquis said sharply.

"I understand," Narda replied humbly.

The Marquis then told her that she would require very little luggage with her and everything else was to be left on board.

He knew as he spoke that no man could have asked for a more attentive and apparently obedient pupil.

At the same time, she looked very lovely as she listened to him.

He could not help wondering if that in itself might not be an added danger.

He told himself, however, that as English tourists they would arouse little interest amongst the ordinary inhabitants of Fez.

Unless, of course, they were prepared to spend money, which was always an "Open Sesame" to an Arab's heart.

"We arrive the day after to-morrow," he finished by saying, "and to-morrow I want to go over with you in detail exactly what we will say and what we will do, so that nothing that happens can take us by surprise."

Narda felt a little shiver run through her.

"I . . . I feel a little frightened."

"There is no need to be frightened," the Marquis said quietly.

"I think . . . that is . . . untrue," she said. "Where I am concerned we are dealing with a . . . devious and . . . unscrupulous man who has stolen a . . . valuable necklace, and I am sure . . . your problem, though different, involves danger."

"That is if I have a problem," the Marquis said.

Narda did not speak, and he said:

"What makes you so positive that I have a secret reason for going to Fez?"

Narda looked away from him, and as she did not speak, he said:

"I am waiting for your answer, Narda."

"I . . . I can read your . . . thoughts," she said.

"If that is true, it is something I very much resent!" the Marquis exclaimed. "But tell me why you are so certain that you can do so."

"It is not . . . something I can do with . . . everybody," she replied. "I think it is . . . actually only with very . . . intelligent people who have . . . unusual and . . . intriguing thoughts which are . . . worth . . . knowing about."

The Marquis's lips tightened, and when he did not speak, she went on:

"I know exactly what your Secretary, Major Ashley, had been told to tell me before he said it, and I knew when you said you were going to Fez that you were going on a secret mission which was very important to somebody, even if not directly to yourself."

There was silence before the Marquis said:

"I find what you are saying very perturbing. All I can beg of you, Narda, if you guess such things, is to keep your guesses to yourself and certainly not to speak of them to anybody else."

"You must be aware that I would not do such a thing," Narda answered.

Now she had lifted her chin, and there was a sharp note in her voice which had not been there before.

"I am quite certain that I can trust you," the Marquis said quietly, "and if you can read my thoughts, then you must know that even to *think* can be dangerous in case other people can read your thoughts."

Narda smiled.

"I have often thought of that, and of course in the Moslem World people are attuned to the 'World

101

Behind the World,' and it is easy for them to be perceptive."

"Then be on your guard!" the Marquis warned. "And if you find yourself thinking of me and what I am hiding from you, then deliberately make yourself think of something else."

"I will try to do that," Narda said. "At the same time, you cannot prevent me from being curious."

"That is one thing you are not to be!" the Marquis said sharply. "And of course one reason why I did not wish to bring anyone with me."

"I understand . . . of course I understand," Narda said. "I promise you that, because you have been so kind and I am very grateful, I will try to be exactly what you want me to be."

She glanced at him from under her eye-lashes before she said:

"You must admit I have been very good up until now by doing exactly what Major Ashley told me you wanted me to do."

"That is true," the Marquis conceded, "and I have been pleasantly surprised by your obedience."

"And now," Narda said, "tell me a little about the Dale family, just in case anyone asks me where we live in England and if our parents are alive, and my answers do not coincide with yours."

* * *

The following evening they went to bed early, and before it was dawn Yates knocked on Narda's cabin door.

She had arranged, the night before, everything she was going to wear and take with her.

She got up and dressed quickly.

The Marquis had impressed upon her the importance of wearing plain, unobtrusive clothes, nothing fanciful that would draw attention to her.

Fortunately the clothes she had with her were simple and at the same time becoming.

When she went up to the Saloon she found the Marquis waiting for her.

He was wearing riding trousers and a jacket which were obviously well-worn and nothing like his usual smart attire.

He had also, Narda noticed, in some clever way altered his personality.

He looked a little older and somewhat scholastic, as an Archaeologist might be expected to look.

He carried a slightly battered suitcase which contained his clothes.

Yates had found one for Narda which she knew was a cheap make, but large enough to hold everything she would require.

She had expected that *The Dolphin* would put into a harbour.

To her surprise, in the distance she could see a high cliff through the darkness.

They were still some way out to sea.

The stars were fading in the sky, while the moon had gone behind a cloud.

When Narda went out on deck with the Marquis, she could see that below them there was a boat with two oarsmen in it.

The Marquis climbed down the rope-ladder first, then, standing in the boat, helped Narda as she joined him.

The seamen started to row away from *The Dolphin*, moving closer to the high cliffs.

They rowed for nearly half-an-hour, and fortunately the sea was calm.

As they went, the dawn came quickly and the sun rose up over the land.

Then almost as if somebody had lit a great candle, the light illuminated the sky and it was day.

It was then Narda could see just a little ahead of them there was a small harbour.

As they neared it, the Marquis said in a low voice as if she had asked the question:

"That is Keniteh. It is the nearest port to Fez."

Narda nodded.

The seamen rowed on until they were inside the harbour.

It was almost deserted, and when they reached a wooden quay, the seamen held the boat steady while the Marquis and Narda stepped ashore.

Without anyone speaking a word, the seamen sa-luted the Marquis and rowed the boat back out to sea.

The Marquis looked around him as they stood with their suitcases beside them.

At last one of the men at the far end of the quay came towards them.

"Want someone help you, *Monsieur*?" he asked.

He spoke in broken French with an Arab accent and the Marquis replied in the same language.

At the same time, he inserted words of Arabic

104

which made it easier for the man to understand.

Narda realised he was asking for animals to carry them to Fez.

He was also explaining that they had arrived in a ship which was going on to Casablanca.

He made it sound very plausible.

The man led them to join a number of other men and they all discussed the Marquis's request.

It took time and a great deal of argument as they haggled over the price.

Narda thought it was clever of the Marquis to say they wanted to inspect some ruins which lay between the port and Fez.

He was still speaking slowly in French with a number of Arab words included.

Finally, when the men understood exactly what he required, the Marquis and Narda walked to the only Inn in sight.

It was clean and obviously used to accommodating travellers.

They asked for breakfast.

The food was plain but edible and they consumed quite a substantial meal.

By the time they had finished, the caravan which the Marquis had ordered arrived to carry them to Fez.

It consisted of two small but spritely Arab horses such as Narda had expected to find in Morocco.

There were also three camels which the Marquis had been told were young and fast-moving.

They had to carry their suitcases and the tents in which they would sleep at night.

Narda realised that it was very wise of the Marquis

to arrive in exactly the way an ordinary Archaeologist would travel.

Carriages, while faster, would travel along the roads.

They would go overland and inspect the ruins in which he was supposed to be so interested.

If anyone was suspicious that he had some other reason for being in Fez, it was obvious he was in no particular hurry to get there.

She knew he was being extremely cautious and would undoubtedly deceive anyone who might be curious about him.

He talked to her in the Hotel and in front of the men accompanying them as if she were very young and, she thought, very stupid.

They rode through the streets of Keniteh with the camels just behind them.

The Marquis pointed out to her a Minaret as if she had never seen one before.

She had a glimpse of low-built houses and a narrow street crowded with beggars and heavily laden donkeys.

There were numerous children playing in the dusty roads.

Then they were outside the town and in the open country.

Narda felt at once it was what she had longed to see, but once her father had died, she thought she would never do so.

When the rough foliage and sparsely leafed trees gave way to barren ground, she felt her heart leap with excitement.

In front of her the desert land drifted away until it joined the sky.

The horse on which she was riding was young and obstreperous.

She, however, forced him to go slower so that she kept pace beside the Marquis.

They were some way ahead of the camels.

Turning his head slightly without appearing to do so, the Marquis said with a smile:

"I took it for granted that as you came from the country you would be able to ride."

"I rode before I could walk!" Narda said. "I cannot tell you how thrilled I am to be on African soil and know I am seeing what I have always wanted to see— the desert!"

The Marquis laughed.

"A very small and inferior one," he said. "The real deserts, as you know, are much farther South."

"But this is what I thought it would be like," Narda said, "and all I want to complete the picture is a Mirage!"

The Marquis laughed again.

"I will try to arrange it," he said dryly. "But of course I make no promises!"

"I am quite prepared to believe you are a Magician," Narda replied, "and it will be humiliating if you disappoint me!"

"Now you are trying to make me do the impossible," the Marquis said, "but, as you well know in these parts, if you believe, the impossible is always possible."

Narda turned her face up towards the sun, and

it was a very lovely gesture.

"I believe . . . of course I believe!" she said. "So how can I doubt for a moment that all my dreams will come true?"

chapter six

THEY rode for a long time.

The ground beneath them became rough with occasional shrubs and, after a little while, quite a number of trees.

Narda looked at them wistfully, wishing they could stop in their shade.

She knew, however, by the expression on the Marquis's face that he was pushing on to the ruins he had said he wished to see.

When they reached them they were most unimpressive.

But he deliberately dismounted and was very voluble in explaining to Narda their significance.

The Arabs in charge of the camels could hear what they were saying.

Narda thought he was acting out his part down to the very last syllable.

They ate the luncheon which they had brought with them under the shade of some trees, and then moved on again.

Narda began to feel tired and rather stiff, as she had not ridden for several weeks.

They reached what appeared to be an oasis of trees, where at last the Marquis conceded that they would stop for the night.

It was inevitable as he and Narda were riding horses that they would reach it first.

She slipped to the ground, realising as she did so that she was more tired than her horse.

She patted him while the Marquis looked to see if there was any water amid the trees for the horses to drink.

They were, however, unlucky.

The horses had to wait until the camels arrived with the huge bladder-containers filled with water which they lapped up eagerly.

The sun was not as hot as it had been earlier in the day.

As Narda pulled off her shady hat there was just a faint breeze which she hoped would increase later.

Two men were erecting their tents and another was unpacking their food.

The Marquis asked sympathetically:

"Are you tired?"

"I am rather," Narda admitted, "but I have enjoyed every second of to-day, and I am so very thrilled to be here."

There was the usual enthusiasm in her voice which he liked.

He sat down on the ground beside her.

He had taken off his jacket and was wearing a silk handkerchief instead of a tie round his neck.

It made him look younger, she thought, and not as awe-inspiring and authoritative as he usually did.

"Tell me about yourself," he invited her. "I find it hard to realise you are so young when you appear to know so much about things which interest me."

"Most of it is second-hand knowledge," Narda admitted, "but I can see pictures of the places described in books, and they become even more clear when people like you and Papa describe them to me."

"We talked a lot about places," the Marquis said, "but what about people?"

"I have tried to study languages so that when I am able to travel I can talk to the people of the country I am in," Narda replied. "I did not like to suggest it when we were on *The Dolphin,* but I wish you would teach me some words of Berber."

"It is a difficult language," the Marquis said.

"You can speak it!" Narda retorted.

He hesitated and she knew he was wondering whether he should admit to being proficient in that language and whether it would be indiscreet to let her be aware of it.

Quickly she said:

"I know you do not want me to ask you questions, and I promise you I am controlling my curiosity with a will of iron!"

The Marquis laughed.

Then he said:

"You are a very unusual young woman, but I trust

you, so I admit I can speak quite a number of languages, and Berber is amongst them."

Narda clapped her hands.

"That is what I thought was the truth," she said, "and I think it is very, very clever of you."

There was silence.

Then she said after a moment:

"Suppose what you are . . . undertaking when we . . . reach Fez is so . . . dangerous that you . . . disappear. What . . . should I . . . do?"

The Marquis looked at her sharply.

Then, as he realised the question was not only a reasonable one but also important, he replied:

"What you suggest will not happen, but if by any chance something did, then you must go at once to the British Consulate and explain who you are. Give them your real name, and not the one on the passport. They will then look after you."

"And . . . what about . . . you?" Narda asked hesitatingly.

"I promise I can look after myself," the Marquis answered firmly.

He rose to his feet as he spoke and walked away to supervise the erection of the tents.

Narda knew that conversation was at an end, and it was something which would not be spoken of again.

At the same time, she sent up a little prayer that he would be safe, and she would not lose him.

'It would be . . . very . . . frightening,' she thought, 'to be here alone . . . in Morocco.'

She knew now that the Marquis had been completely right when he had said that she could not travel to this strange land alone.

"But I had to come!" she said beneath her breath as if she must defend herself.

She watched him as he stood talking to the camel-drivers.

He was speaking to them in the same mixture of French and Arab that he had used in Keniteh.

"He is being very careful," she told herself, "and I am sure, whatever he says, that there is danger waiting for him in Fez."

They ate their dinner before the sun went down.

The Marquis had bought a bottle of wine at the Inn where they had had breakfast.

Then, as the first evening star appeared overhead, he said:

"I think we would be wise to go to bed now and rise early so that we can do a large part of our journey to-morrow, while it is still cool."

"I am sure that is sensible," Narda agreed.

She got to her feet, and as the Marquis did the same, she looked up at him.

"Thank you . . . thank you," she said in a soft voice, "for bringing me with . . . you. I was thinking a little while ago that I would have been very . . . frightened if I had come here . . . alone."

"Of course you would," the Marquis said. "I can only hope your journey is rewarded by your finding what you seek."

"Even if I am unable to do so," Narda said, "I will never forget or regret that I have been to Morocco."

She paused, then before the Marquis could speak she added:

"So I can only . . . once again say 'thank you.'"

The sun that was just beginning to sink over the horizon illuminated her face.

There seemed to be a touch of silver in the fairness of her hair.

She looked so lovely that the Marquis suddenly had an almost uncontrollable desire to kiss her.

It was what he would have done with any other woman.

He had only to stretch out his arms and pull her close to him.

Then with an effort he realised that she was still speaking to him as if he were some much older person she could trust.

In her large eyes looking up into his there was the expression with which he was so familiar. The Marquis turned away.

"Good-night, Narda," he said, "and sleep well."

"I shall do that," she answered, "and I am sure the spirits of the trees are watching over us."

Once again she was speaking in that dreamy voice that she had used when she was looking for the mermaids.

As he went towards his tent, the Marquis was sure that the spirits of the trees were very real to her.

The two tents had been erected some distance from each other.

Narda's was the smaller of the two.

In fact, it was a single tent in which it was impossible to stand upright.

The Marquis's was larger, and he wondered as he went into it if he should offer it to Narda.

Then he knew that that would be a mistake in a land where women were totally subservient to men.

The camels and their drivers were some way away from them under another clump of trees.

They had lit a fire over which they were preparing some special food of their own.

They had their mats on which to sit and which also served as bedding when they lay down to sleep.

The Marquis was aware that these particular camel-drivers made the journey regularly from Keniteh to Fez.

He was sure they were familiar with every inch of the land.

Doubtless, therefore, this was a place at which they usually stopped for the night.

Darkness had come with its habitual swiftness.

He undressed, and when he got into bed, the stars were coming out.

The first rays of the moonlight were seeping through the trees overhead.

*   *   *

Narda was also in bed.

She was thinking how exciting it was to be sleeping, as she had always wanted to do, in the desert.

She had often talked about it with her father.

He had said to her frankly that he was too old to require anything but a comfortable bed and proper washing facilities.

"You have been spoilt, Papa!" she teased him.

"I have travelled cheaply and also luxuriously," her

father replied, "and frankly, I prefer the latter."

They had both laughed at the time, but now Narda knew that one of her dreams had come true.

She said her prayers.

Then because she in fact was very tired after such a long ride in the heat of the day, her eyes closed.

She fell asleep.

*　　*　　*

Narda awoke with a start because she felt something hard and rather rough across her mouth.

She opened her eyes, but there was only darkness.

Then she was aware that something strange and horrifying was happening to her.

She could not for a moment imagine what was over her mouth, but it was being tightened until it hurt.

When she tried to struggle, something thick was pulled over her head and dragged down over her shoulders.

It pinioned her arms to her sides.

She tried frantically to free herself, but could feel her legs being tied together at the ankles.

She was pulled backwards and realised in terror that she was being taken out of the tent through the back of it.

It was all happening without a sound.

Although she tried to scream, it was impossible because of the gag over her mouth.

Then she was picked up, she thought, by two men.

Another held her feet, and she knew she was being carried away.

They moved so silently that she could not hear their footsteps.

She feared that neither the Marquis nor the camel-drivers would be aware of what was happening.

She was so tightly bound that it was impossible to move.

She could only remain stiff as she was carried what seemed to her an incredibly long distance.

Then at last they set her down, not on the ground but in what she thought was a vehicle of some sort.

Because she was so frightened, it was difficult to think.

Then she was moved again, this time onto a seat.

Because it had been getting harder and harder to breathe, it was a relief when what had covered her head was pulled off.

Her arms were released at the same time.

She thought as the thick material was moved away from her eyes that she would be able to see.

Instead, she found she was in darkness.

She tried to breathe in what air there was, longing to gasp, but unable to do so because of the gag.

The men who had carried her moved away in the darkness.

Then to her surprise she felt wheels beneath her beginning to turn.

She knew that the vehicle in which she had been placed was moving.

She put up her hands, hoping to find something to hold on to.

To her astonishment, she found she was touching the arm of somebody sitting next to her.

It was such a shock that she quickly took her hand away.

A moment later she heard the voice of a woman whispering quietly into her ear:

"Keep still. Do not move or make a fuss, or they will drug you!"

Narda could hardly believe what she heard was true.

Yet she was aware that the hair of the woman who had spoken to her had brushed against her cheek.

Automatically she did as the woman said and ceased to struggle or try to move.

Anyway, it was very difficult with her feet tied.

Then she realised that her hands were free.

She lifted them up, feeling at the back of her head for the knot which tied the gag over her mouth.

With a little difficulty she managed to undo it.

Then, when she had removed it from her mouth, she could gasp for air as she had wanted to do.

It had taken a little time, and now the wheels were moving more quickly.

Through the noise she heard the woman next to her say:

"They have kidnapped you, but keep very quiet."

"Why have they . . . done such a . . . thing?" Narda asked in a whisper. "Who are . . . they?"

She thought the woman next to her was about to answer, when suddenly ahead there was a glint of light.

It came, Narda knew, from behind the driver's seat of the vehicle, and she realised that a man was looking back at them.

She felt the woman beside her stiffen and instinctively did the same.

She could only just faintly make out the outline of his head, but she thought he was looking to see how she was behaving.

She was afraid he would come back and replace the gag over her mouth.

She was very still except that she dropped her head forward just in case he could see her clearly.

He seemed to look towards her for what she felt was a long time.

Actually, it was the passing of only a few seconds.

Then he turned and there was darkness again.

Because she was so frightened, she reached out towards the woman next to her and found her hand.

The woman's fingers closed over hers, and it was comforting.

Narda turned her head towards her.

"Please . . . tell me . . . what is . . . happening," she begged. "I . . . I am so . . . frightened!"

"So am I," the woman admitted, "but there is nothing we can do until we reach Fez."

She now realised that it was not an older woman sitting beside her, but a girl, probably no older than herself.

"We are going to Fez?" Narda asked.

She thought that, at any rate, was a comfort.

The Marquis, when he knew she was missing, would undoubtedly go there first.

The girl holding her hand moved a little nearer to her.

"I heard them say they would steal you," she said,

"because one of the girls in this lot had jumped overboard when they were asleep."

"Why did she do . . . that?" Narda enquired.

"Because she realised what was going to happen to
us," the girl beside her answered.

Narda's fingers tightened on hers.

"What *is* going to . . . happen to . . . us?" she
asked.

There was a little pause before the girl beside her
said:

"It will frighten you, but perhaps it is better if you
know the worst."

"Tell . . . me," Narda pleaded.

"These men are procurers of girls for the Arabs!"

Narda gave a little gasp.

She remembered hearing her father saying when
they were in Constantinople that there was a constant
trade in European girls taken to Turkey.

They filled the Harems of the Sultan and wealthy
Turks.

For a moment she was unable to speak.

Then she asked in a terror-stricken little voice:

"Are you . . . are you talking . . . about the . . .
White Slave Traffic?"

"Yes, I am," the girl replied, "and I was caught by
an old trick."

"What was . . . that?"

"I answered an advertisement for a Nursery Governess who was prepared to travel."

There was a little sob in her voice as she went on:

"How could I have been so . . . foolish as not
to . . . guess there was something . . . strange about

120

it when the man . . . interviewed me?"

She gave another sob and went on:

"He said I was accepted for the post and the lady who had engaged me would be waiting with the children I was to teach when I reached Morocco."

"You had no . . . idea that you . . . were being . . . deceived?" Narda asked.

"It never entered my head," the girl said. "My name is Elsie Watson and my father is the Vicar of a parish in Gloucestershire. It sounded so exciting to be able to see the world."

"I can understand that," Narda agreed, "and are there . . . other girls . . . here?"

She had noticed as Elsie was talking that they were sitting on the third row of seats in the cart.

She was almost certain there were other girls present, although they were making no sound.

As if she had asked the question, Elsie said:

"They are drugged. It is only because I have eaten and drunk nothing since we landed that I am not in the same condition."

"They . . . drugged the . . . food?" Narda asked in horror.

"The food and also the drink," Elsie answered. "They did so on board the ship with anyone who made a fuss, especially after the girl who realised what was happening threw herself into the sea."

Narda drew in her breath, but she did not speak, and Elsie went on:

"I knew then that if I am to escape, as I intend to do, I had to pretend to believe everything they said."

"What . . . did they . . . say?"

"They just said the woman was hysterical and that we all had the positions waiting for us in Fez which they had promised when we were engaged."

"How . . . how many . . . girls are . . . there here?" Narda enquired.

"We were nine until they kidnapped you because they were afraid they would get into trouble from the men who gave them their orders when we reach Fez."

"But surely they expect . . . the . . . person with whom I am . . . travelling to make . . . a fuss?"

She hesitated because she had nearly said "the Marquis," then remembered who she was supposed to be.

"I understood what was happening," Elsie said, "because they were speaking in French. It was when I heard the Frenchmen talking on board that I realised what they really were."

"What did . . . they say . . . about me?" Narda asked.

"They watched as your tent was erected under the trees and they said you were young and pretty and had only one man to protect you."

"But . . . the camel-drivers . . . " Narda began.

"They would not interfere," Elsie said. "I gather the man who is the head of this evil trade is of great importance. I expect most people in Fez would be too frightened to oppose him in any way."

Narda felt her heart sink.

Then she told herself that the Marquis was different.

He too was of great importance, and she was sure that somehow he would save her.

At the same time, she was terrified in case he could not do so.

How could she help him if she was drugged like the eight girls lying silently in the other seats?

"Help me . . . please help me . . . " she whispered to Elsie.

"I will try to," Elsie said, "just as I am trying to help myself, but it is not going to be easy."

"How many . . . men are . . . there carrying . . . us?" Narda enquired.

"There are six," Elsie replied. "Whatever happens, you must not try to run away. They will drug you or beat you. They kidnapped you because they themselves are so afraid of the anger they will arouse if their consignment is short by one girl!"

Narda realised that even to try to run away in the circumstances would be very foolish.

At the same time, every instinct within her cried out that she must do something, anything, rather than suffer the fate of European girls who had been taken to Turkey.

Because she read the newspapers assiduously, she had seen references to the horror and degradation of the White Slave Traffic.

Now that she thought about it, she could remember reading how in Australia they had stopped it.

Those who procured the girls were sentenced to at least ten years in prison and were flogged at regular intervals while they were there.

There had been questions in Parliament as to why the same steps should not be taken in England.

Yet as far as she knew, nothing had been done.

English girls, like those from a number of other countries in Europe, were continually being shipped to the Arab world.

"What they like," Elsie was saying, "are girls with fair hair, which I am sure is what you have."

"Yes . . . I am . . . fair," Narda admitted.

"So am I," Elsie answered. "Why, oh, why did I ever wish to leave Papa and travel abroad?"

"It is . . . cruel and wicked that . . . we should be . . . caught up in anything so . . . horrible!" Narda said. "I am sure, as your father is a parson, you know the only thing we can do is to pray."

"That is what I have been doing," Elsie said. "I have prayed until I thought that not only God but all the angels in Heaven must have heard my cries for help! But so far I am still travelling to my doom!"

"We . . . have to . . . believe," Narda said, and she was speaking to herself as much as to Elsie.

With a little sob Elsie said:

"You are quite right . . . there is nothing else we can do."

They were silent for some time.

Then Elsie said:

"You have not told me your name and what you are doing in Morocco."

"My name is Narda, and I am with my . . . b-brother, who is an Archaeologist. He will not . . . allow me to just . . . disappear."

"If they are as clever at abducting you as they were at collecting all of us," Elsie said, "no one will have the slightest idea where you have gone, or what has happened to you."

"You do not . . . think the . . . camel-drivers will tell my brother?"

"They would be too frightened," Elsie replied. "The men with us are well-spoken, and what you might call of good class. But I know from the way they behaved when the girl drowned herself that they are scared to death of their master, whoever he may be!"

"It could not be . . . the Sultan," Narda said.

"We shall never know until we are confronted with him," Elsie replied.

"I want to scream and scream," Narda said, "but I suppose nobody would hear me, and it would do . . . . no good."

"They will simply render you unconscious in one way or another," Elsie replied. "If we have the slightest chance of escaping, we must be ready and alert at any moment to do so."

"Yes . . . of course," Narda replied.

She thought for a moment. Then she asked:

"Do you think it will be all right for me to remove the rope from around my ankles? It is so tight that it hurts."

"I will do it for you," Elsie said. "As long as you do not try to run away, they may not notice that you are free."

She crouched down as she spoke and undid the heavy rope which secured Narda's ankles together.

When she had done so Narda said:

"Thank you . . . thank you. If you were not here, I think I should have died of fright! It is so comforting to have somebody who is English to talk to."

"The others are mostly English," Elsie said. "Three

125

of them are country girls of about fifteen who came to London to look for domestic employment in one of the great houses."

"The poor things!" Narda exclaimed.

"Two want to go on the stage," Elsie went on, "and I suspect they would have got into trouble anyway. The rest, like myself, answered advertisements in the newspapers."

"What did the advertisement say?" Narda asked.

"That there was a good position abroad as governess, lady's-maid, or shop-assistant," Elsie replied. "They still have no idea of what will happen when they reach Fez."

"How long do you think it will take us to get there?" Narda asked nervously.

"From what I heard them say, they expect to be there to-morrow afternoon," Elsie replied. "This cart is drawn by four horses and can move quite quickly."

Narda's hopes faded.

She thought there was no chance of the Marquis reaching Fez as soon as that.

Then she knew it would be possible if he left the camels and rode ahead to Fez.

She closed her eyes and sent out her thoughts towards him, telling him where she was.

Then she thought he would be still asleep and it was too soon to try to contact him.

He would not know until it was dawn that she had been taken from him.

She made an involuntary sound of despair and Elsie said:

"Cheer up! As we both believe in God, we have to believe that He knows the predicament we are in and will hear our cry for help."

"I am . . . sure He . . . will," Narda said, "and so will my brother."

At the same time, she knew in her heart that it was only the Marquis who could save her.

Somehow, by some means, she must help him to realise where she was and what had happened to her.

* * *

The Marquis must have been asleep for two hours.

Suddenly he awoke and was aware with the alertness of a man used to danger that there was somebody inside his tent.

"Who is there?" he asked sharply in French.

Then he saw silhouetted against the opening which he had left uncovered, there was the figure of a man.

He repeated the question, this time in Berber.

The man moved a little nearer to him and went down on his knees.

The Marquis instinctively reached for the loaded revolver under his pillow.

"I tell bad news, Master, important news," the man said. "But I poor man, earn very little looking after my goats."

He spoke in a way that was difficult to understand.

But the Marquis was experienced in dealing with difficult dialects, and he asked:

"If you have something of importance to tell me, then you will be rewarded."

He thought the man was pleased, and after a moment he said:

"Young girl taken away. I see her go."

The Marquis stiffened.

"What did you see?"

"Three men take young girl from tent, put her in a big cart."

"I cannot imagine what you are talking about," the Marquis said.

At the same time, he got out of bed.

Without troubling to put anything over his nightshirt, he walked out of the tent towards Narda's.

One look at where the back had been skilfully cut open told him how they had done it.

He returned to his tent and felt for the bag of money he had also placed beneath his pillow.

He took out a number of coins and put them into the man's hand.

The goatherd had not moved since the Marquis had left him, and now he sat back on his heels and said:

"Men take woman silently. No one hear sounds."

"The camel-drivers should have been aware they were there!" the Marquis insisted.

"They sleep. Want no trouble," the man replied.

"What was the cart like in which they took the girl away?" the Marquis asked.

"Big—very big, four horses," the man replied.

"How many men?"

"Three carry girl—three stay in cart."

"Have you any idea who they are?" the Marquis asked.

The man nodded.

"Meet ship often. Bring girls to Fez."

Now the Marquis knew exactly what he was up against and what had happened to Narda.

He paid the man generously for what he had told him.

He waited until he was safely out of sight with his goats before he aroused the camel-drivers.

He knew only too well that if the goatherd was identified as informing against those organising the White Slave Traffic, he would not live long.

"My sister could have joined some other cameldrivers," he said vaguely, "and gone on ahead of us to Fez. I must therefore follow her as quickly as possible."

He told them where to take his suitcases and promised them they would be well paid for for doing so.

He put his saddle on Narda's horse, thinking that as hers was younger, it would be the less tired of the two.

As he rode off, he knew that he had to rescue her.

Every nerve in his body was straining to think of how he should do so.

He rode very quickly for quite a long time.

He had realised at once that if he found Narda and learnt who had abducted her, he would at the same time have found the answer for which Lord Derby was waiting.

But as he rode on he told himself that it was Narda who mattered.

She mattered to him, but he had not admitted it to himself until that moment.

"I will save her," he vowed, "if I have to kill every damned man in Fez to do so!"

chapter seven

DAWN had broken and it was daylight before the vehicle came to a standstill.

"What is . . . happening?" Narda asked in a whisper.

"I think they are changing the horses," Elsie answered. "Pretend to be asleep or they will drug you."

Although her heart was beating frantically, Narda forced herself to shut her eyes.

She leant back with her head dropping forward, as if she were asleep.

She was aware that a man came to look at the rest of the passengers.

She knew, as Elsie had said, that there were eight other women in the cart.

She had been able to see them in the light which came through the sides of the cart.

It was covered completely with a coarse canvas.

The passengers were seated in quite comfortable chairs which had been arranged four in a row.

The girls were slumped down in them and were so silent that Narda thought it was eerie.

Now a man pulled back the canvas on one side of the cart.

She longed to look at him and see what sort of person he was.

But she was wise enough to know that her only hope of being able to escape was to do everything that Elsie told her.

The man stood in the opening for some time before he was joined by another.

"They all right?" the newcomer asked sharply in French.

"Seem so," the first man replied.

"What about the last girl? Did you drug her?"

"No need," the first man replied. "I haven't heard a sound from her since we put her in with the others."

Narda drew in her breath.

She knew that both men were looking at her.

It was with the greatest difficulty that she forced her hands to appear relaxed.

"She's taken off the gag!" the second man exclaimed.

"If she wakes, give her something to drink. We don't want trouble when we reach Fez."

Even as he spoke, one of the girls in the front seat stirred and woke up.

"Where . . . am . . . I?" she asked piteously. "Where are . . . we going?"

"See to her!" the second man said sharply.

The first man at once climbed into the cart.

"You're all right," he said soothingly in quite passable English. "You soon be in Fez and people from theatre waiting for you."

"I . . . I am frightened . . . I want to . . . go home!" the girl wailed.

"That's foolish," the man said. "You be a big success, everyone applaud you. What you need is drink. This delicious! Drink it and you feel better."

Although Narda did not look, she knew he had given the girl a glass of something.

"Drink it all," he said encouragingly. "Be hot later and you feel thirsty."

The girl obviously obeyed him.

Then he said:

"Now go sleep and forget everything but success you be when you dance."

The girl murmured something before she slumped back in her chair.

After waiting for a few seconds to see if she would speak again, the man climbed out of the cart and secured the flap at the side.

The cart was now covered completely again, and only as the new horses moved off did Elsie say:

"He handled that efficiently. You do understand that if we eat or drink anything, we will lose our wits?"

"I am . . . thirsty," Narda said, "but of course you are right."

"I have hardly dared to eat anything since we left England," Elsie said. "As soon as I realised what they were doing I remembered what my father had told me about the White Slave Traffic, and . . . I know how . . . horrifying it . . . is!"

Her voice shook as she spoke.

Narda took hold of her hand again and pressed it.

"I am sure my . . . brother will somehow manage to save us,"

"We can only hope so," Elsie replied, "but how is he to know where you are?"

Narda did not answer.

She was only hoping that she was right in thinking the Marquis knew people who would know the secrets of Fez.

He could turn to them for help.

They had gone a long way before she asked Elsie the question that was uppermost in her mind.

"If . . . we are . . . not rescued, what . . . shall we . . . do?"

There was a pause before Elsie replied:

"I intend to . . . kill myself. I am not . . . certain how . . . but I shall . . . find a . . . way."

"I must do . . . the same," Narda murmured.

Even as she spoke she knew she did not want to die.

She wanted to find the Marquis again, to talk to him, and above all, to be with him.

"Oh, God . . . help me!" she prayed. "I want . . . to live . . . and if I die . . . he will never . . . know where I am or what . . . has happened to . . . me!"

*   *   *

When they reached Fez it was evening and darkness had already fallen.

Although behind the canvas they could see nothing, Narda was aware they had reached the City.

She could hear the noise in the streets and the clatter of the horses' hooves on the cobble-stones.

Narda knew that Elsie was tense, thinking that perhaps this was the moment when they might escape.

The horses drew to a standstill.

A man climbed into the cart and said:

"Wake up, girls! We arrive and there's people waiting to meet you!"

The drugs must have been wearing off.

Yet some of the girls who had been drugged for a long time did not seem to want to talk.

They looked around them as if bewildered, and the pupils of their eyes were dilated.

It had been difficult to see clearly what they were like.

Narda now saw that every one of them, just like herself and Elsie, had fair hair.

She knew that because the Arabs were themselves dark, they liked fair women.

Even to think of it made her shiver.

Now the man who was giving orders made two of the girls in front stand up.

Another man handed up to him long yellow *djellabas* which were worn by most of the people in Fez.

They had peaked hoods which covered their heads and most of their faces.

It made it impossible to tell whether they were a man or a woman.

When the man had dressed each girl, who seemed too limp to do anything for herself, he pushed her to the opening of the cart.

Then she was lifted to the ground.

Outside, there was light from a flare near the entrance to show what was happening.

Narda could see a man marching the first girl away while another man reached for the next one.

Because she was at the back of the cart there was only one girl to follow after she and Elsie had left.

She did not pretend to be limp and dazed as the other girls had been.

The man—and Narda was sure it was the same one who had spoken to the girl he had drugged—put a pointed hood over her head.

He buttoned her *djellaba* down the front.

Then he pushed her towards the opening and she was lifted down by a man standing outside.

He moved off, holding her by the arm.

She saw they were in a narrow street in which there were a few shops or booths still open.

The night air seemed to be full of the rhythmic hammerings of iron-workers, who she knew were labouring on their kettles.

They must also have passed a coppersmith's because she could hear the tip-tapping on their ornate trays.

She had seen this when she had been with her father, and she recognised what they were doing.

Now, as she was taken farther away from the cart, there seemed to be more people in the road.

There were the rasping cries of the street vendors.

Donkeys were being driven by men who shouted: *"Valek, valek!"* which meant "Make way."

Narda had been in the streets of Constantinople and Cairo.

She therefore recognised the aroma of spices, newly-cut cedarwood, and sizzling hot cooking-oil.

On they walked, and she hated the greasy stones on which she slipped in her bare feet.

Then at last the man walking beside her stopped abruptly.

She found herself pushed through a door which closed immediately behind them.

It was dark, but he went ahead, pulling her after him.

Unexpectedly they were in a court-yard with a fountain in the middle which was not playing.

There was the scent of flowers.

Narda could see by the light of several lanterns that it was luxurious with a flooring of mosaics and marble tiles.

It obviously belonged to somebody who was rich.

The man escorting her did not speak.

They moved through the court-yard, through another door, and up some stairs.

He drew aside a curtain.

Now they were in a large room with divans and pillow-like cushions set on a richly woven carpet.

The other girls were there already, sitting, as if they were too limp to stand up.

Most of them were staring into space in a dazed fashion.

Because she thought it wise, Narda tried to behave in the same way.

She let the man who had escorted her take off her peaked *djellaba*.

Then he pushed her down onto a divan.

She stayed in one position, as if she were too limp to do anything else.

To her relief, she saw Elsie being brought into the room.

Because there was nobody else on the divan, Elsie sat down beside her.

A few minutes later the last girl, who was in a worse state than the others, was carried into the room.

She was put down in a corner with cushions at her back.

She was too drugged to move.

The man who had brought her in said to the man who had followed them:

"That's the lot."

The man to whom he was speaking looked around.

Then he said in French:

"Give them food and drink, and I'll notify the Master they're here."

He left the room as servants came in, carrying trays of food.

There were deep-baked chickens and a steaming mountain of cous-cous.

There were chunks of lamb with yellow beans and a dish of semolina.

On a number of small plates there were the inevitable olives, nuts, yoghourt, sweetbreads, and Moroccan bread.

Because she was both hungry and thirsty, Narda felt her mouth watering.

"Be careful!" Elsie said in a whisper.

"You . . . mean that we eat . . . nothing?" Narda asked.

She was not looking at Elsie as she spoke but watching the man standing inside the room.

He appeared to be looking at the servants.

They were setting out the dishes on a long, low table in the centre of the carpet.

"Fruit, only fruit," Elsie warned her.

For a moment Narda thought there was none.

Then to her relief she saw a servant bring in a wide basket.

It contained figs, pomegranates, and a number of other fruits.

The servants having finished, the man who had been watching them said in a loud voice in English:

"Come along, girls! I sure you hungry, when you eaten you have mint tea which delicious."

Narda guessed they were keeping that until the end because it was the most heavily drugged.

She longed to sample some of the food.

She would have eagerly eaten the chicken and the lamb.

But she knew that Elsie was right.

If there was any chance of their escaping, it would be when the men in charge of them thought they were drugged.

Slowly, because they found it difficult to move, the girls went to the table.

Narda and Elsie did the same.

Had they been Arabs, they would have sat down cross-legged, but as it was, they crouched.

Because the girls bent forward over the table, it was easy for Elsie to take two figs and two pomegranates from the basket.

She put them in front of Narda and herself.

They certainly helped to quench Narda's thirst.

She was glad to find there were also a few small bananas.

She was certain it would be impossible to drug them.

The man in charge was obviously bored, and he yawned several times.

It was only when the girls had eaten quite a lot that he said:

"Now I send for mint tea. After that you have good sleep until to-morrow."

There was a note in his voice that made Narda aware that to-morrow was important.

Just at that moment men could be heard talking outside.

As if somebody had called him, the man in the room went through the curtain.

"What is . . . happening?" Narda asked.

"It will be to-morrow that the Buyers come," Elsie said, "unless somebody has arrived to-night."

As she spoke, the man who had been watching them came hastily back into the room followed by the servants.

On his instructions, they picked up everything that remained of the meal.

Some of the girls tried to protest as the plates were taken from them before they had finished.

The table on which the food had stood was covered with an embroidered cloth.

As the servants left, the man said sharply:

"Now tidy yourselves. Someone here who wish to meet you."

He spoke in English, but again with a pronounced accent.

The girls, who having eaten had brightened up, stared at him.

Then one of them said:

"I am . . . tired! I want . . . to go to . . . sleep."

"You can sleep later," the man said sharply. "Tidy your hair, look presentable."

She did not seem to understand.

She moved back to the cushion where she had sat before the food had been brought in.

Elsie drew Narda towards the divan.

It was at the end of the room.

There was therefore a number of girls between them and the entrance.

The sound of voices outside grew louder.

Then the man who spoke French came into the room.

Following him was a very large Arab.

He was wearing a white caftan which covered him like a *djellaba*.

At his waist was a long, curved dagger in a gold sheath, its handle decorated with jewels.

He wore a turban and had a grey-flecked beard. On his feet were pointed yellow slip-ons, or *ba-bouches*.

Elsie had stiffened because she knew why he was there.

Narda shut her eyes because she was frightened.

Then she heard the man who spoke French say in Berber:

"It is a very great honour, Abd-Al-Hasan, to receive you!"

She did not understand the language he spoke.

But she sensed from what he said and the tone of his voice that the Arab was of consequence.

The Arab replied:

"My Master very interested in your wares."

As he spoke in a Berber which seemed softer than any she had heard previously, Narda thought she must be dreaming.

She had heard that voice before.

She knew it, and she knew too that every instinct in her body responded to it.

'I must be going mad!' she thought. 'Or else the figs were drugged!'

Then as the man addressed as Abd-Al-Hasan spoke again, she knew she was not mistaken.

How could she be when she could read his thoughts and she knew it was the Marquis!

Now she could understand what he was saying even though she could not speak the language.

He was asking if the girls, who he understood had just been brought from England, were virgins and had not been touched or interfered with on the voyage.

The man who had brought them assured him that they were exactly that.

No man had touched them in any way since they had been in his care.

"My Master is very particular!" Abd-Al-Hasan said. "If you deceive him, he will never patronise you again!"

"I assure you, Honoured Sir, I promise you I tell

the truth!" the Arab said. "Is that not so, Idris?"

He turned to the other man who had been in charge of the cart.

"Yes, yes, Yusuf, that is so."

Yusuf began to point out the attractions of the girls.

He took hold of the nearest and stood her on the table.

Narda understood him to say that if Abd-Al-Hasan wished, she could be undressed.

He was told it was unnecessary, and another girl took her place.

One after another, the bearded Abd-Al-Hasan examined them closely.

He looked at their hands, their faces, and Yusuf pointed out that they had good teeth or small, curved breasts.

One by one they were taken from where they were sitting, stood on the table, then another girl took their place.

Narda felt herself tremble.

She was next.

Because she had been abducted from her tent in the middle of the night, she was still wearing only her nightgown.

She was warm enough because it had been almost stifling in the cart during the day.

Even after her *djellaba* was taken from her she was warm enough in this room which seemed to have no ventilation.

Yusuf put out his hand to drag her towards the table.

Abd-Al-Hasan, who was beside him, raised his

hand and prevented him from doing so.

"I can see that she is young and pretty," he said.

As he spoke, his eyes met Narda's, and she knew she was not mistaken.

It was the Marquis.

With the greatest effort she did not throw herself into his arms and beg him to save her.

Instead, she clasped her hands so that her nails dug into her skin.

She forced herself to turn her head away, as if she were shy.

Then she felt the Marquis's hand on her cheek.

"Soft white skin," he said in Berber.

Because he was touching her, she felt a streak of lightning run through her breasts.

It was so ecstatic that she knew in that moment that she loved him.

He moved on.

Because Narda knew she must save Elsie, she put out her hand and slipped her arms through hers.

It was a gesture any girl might have made.

But she was willing the Marquis to understand that Elsie was special and if it was possible he must buy her too.

There were no more girls to be seen, and now the Marquis asked:

"Is that all?"

"All for the moment, Most Honoured Sir," Yusuf replied, "but we will have another consignment in the near future."

The Marquis made an impatient gesture with his hand.

"I will inform my Master. But for the moment we are concerned with these. Where can we sit down?"

Yusuf led him to the other end of the room, where there were two large cushions and a small table beside them.

Narda sat down again on the divan and watched the bargaining begin.

She knew only the Marquis could have been so clever.

He made it seem entirely natural that he should bargain over every girl.

He complained that Yusuf was asking too much for one because her neck was too thick, for another because her hands were coarse.

Narda felt she could understand everything he was saying.

At the same time, she was aware that he was not deliberately singling her out in case it should arouse suspicion.

Finally, after what seemed an incredibly long time, the Marquis drew from somewhere on his person a large bag of money.

She could see it contained a great number of gold coins.

He placed quite a pile of them on the table before Yusuf.

She was certain that Yusuf's eyes were glinting with greed.

She saw his hand go out like a claw to catch hold of the money.

The bag was almost empty when the Marquis rose to his feet.

He looked across the room towards Narda and said something which for the moment she did not understand.

Idris, who had been listening while Yusuf had been bargaining, came towards her.

Then she understood.

"You two go with important man," he said in English. "You behave well, do what he say. If not, he punish you."

He spoke ferociously, but Narda's heart was singing.

Then, as the Marquis went ahead of them without appearing to be in the least interested, Idris pushed them after him.

They went down the steps to the ground floor.

Instead of leaving by the way they had come through the court-yard, the Marquis, escorted by Yusuf, went along several narrow, twisting corridors.

They passed through another court-yard which was hung with washing.

The tiled floor was cracked and broken.

The house on the other side of it was obviously inhabited by poor and somewhat inferior people.

Still they walked on, the two girls following.

Then a door opened and Narda was aware of the night air on her face.

Outside, in what appeared to be an almost deserted street, there was a carriage.

It was impressive and drawn by two horses.

The Marquis stepped into it, Yusuf bowing as he did so and thanking him profusely for his patronage.

The two girls were pushed in after him and told to sit on the small seat with their backs to the horses.

The door was closed.

The carriage drove off while the two Arabs salaamed as they drove away.

It was difficult to see.

The road up which they were driving had only an occasional light outside the door of a closed shop.

The Marquis did not speak, so Narda was silent.

Only when they had driven for quite some minutes did Elsie say in a frightened whisper:

"I wonder where . . . he is . . . taking us?"

"It is quite all right," the Marquis said in English. "Do not be frightened. But we are not yet out of the wood, and it is best to say as little as possible."

Elsie gave a stifled cry.

"You are English!"

"I am English!" the Marquis replied, "and I have saved you both. What is your name?"

"Elsie Watson."

"Now, listen, Elsie," he said, "when the carriage stops, there will be a man to take you to the British Consulate. You will be safe there and they will have you taken back to England. Until you are out of this country, you must understand that yours, Narda's, and my life are in danger."

"You will . . . save the other . . . girls?" Narda asked.

"They will be collected to-morrow," the Marquis answered, "After that, all hell will break loose, and we shall have to put a great many miles between us and Fez."

As he was speaking in a very low voice the carriage came to a standstill.

Somebody opened the door and the Marquis got out.

Narda saw that outside there were two horses and two men in charge of them.

The Marquis, however, took her by the hand and drew her to where there was a wooden hut.

In the starlight, and there was also light from the moon, she could see they were on rough ground outside the walls of Fez.

As the Marquis and Narda walked into the hut, the carriage drove away.

It seemed to Narda it was going back the way they had come.

Elsie followed them, and inside the hut there was a small, lighted room.

The windows had been shuttered.

"There is food for you," the Marquis said, "and some strong coffee. I was praying you would not be drugged."

"Elsie . . . saved me from . . . that!" Narda cried.

The Marquis looked towards Elsie.

"I am very grateful to you," he said. "I promise you will be properly looked after, but I want you to leave at once. It is most important that no one should know where we have gone or what is happening until the rest of the girls are rescued. Do you understand?"

"Yes . . . of course," Elsie agreed, "and . . . thank you . . . thank you!"

For the first time since Narda had met her, Elsie was crying.

Tears were running down her cheeks.

Narda knew they were tears of relief and happiness because she had been rescued and now would not have to kill herself.

"Narda and I will get in touch with you as soon as we reach England," the Marquis said, "but, because every moment we stay here we are in danger, I want you to go."

Narda put her arms round Elsie and kissed her.

"Thank you . . . thank you," Elsie cried again.

It was difficult for her to speak through her tears.

A man came into the hut.

He carried a dark *burnouse* over his arm which every Moslem woman wears.

The Marquis took it from him and put it over Elsie's head.

"Shuffle along beside him," he said, "as if you are a Moorish woman, and do not say a word until you are in the Consulate."

Elsie nodded because it was impossible for her to speak.

Clutching the *burnouse* around her, she went out of the door and the Marquis shut it.

"Now, hurry!" he said to Narda. "And you can eat as you dress."

"I can do . . . anything . . . now that I am . . . with you!" Narda replied.

She went to the table and put some food into her mouth.

Then she saw that on a chair beside it there were some clothes.

She pulled off her nightgown.

As she did so she realised that the Marquis had gone to another corner of the room and had his back to her.

She dressed hurriedly.

He had provided her with underclothes, and a riding-skirt with a jacket which covered a white blouse.

There was also a pair of short riding-boots like the ones she had worn when she left the yacht.

They were not her own, as none of the other things were.

But they fitted her fairly well except that the boots were slightly too big.

Then, as she turned round to take something else to eat, she saw that the Marquis had discarded his beard and the rest of his disguise.

He was wearing the riding-clothes he had worn when he left the yacht.

"Drink some coffee," he said.

"I would rather have something thirst-quenching," Narda answered. "I have been desperately thirsty, but Elsie warned me against eating or drinking anything in case it was drugged."

"I expected that," the Marquis said, "but I had not anticipated you would be lucky enough to find some-body as sensible as Elsie to tell you what to do."

"She was very, very kind," Narda said, "and I was . . . afraid you would not . . . rescue her with me."

"They will all be rescued to-morrow," the Marquis promised, "unless something goes wrong. But come, we must hurry."

Realising there was nothing else to drink except coffee which, as the Marquis had said, was very strong, Narda gulped it down.

Then she followed him to the door.

Two horses were just outside.

She was relieved to see that the Marquis had provided her with a side-saddle as well as a fresh young horse.

He was prancing and fidgeting, obviously delighted to be able to stretch his legs.

The Marquis waited only to press a large number of coins into the hands of the man who held them.

He *salaamed*, and they rode off.

The Marquis obviously knew the way.

At first they moved between a number of huts of the type in which they had just changed and eaten.

Then, quicker than it seemed possible, the walls of Fez were left behind.

They were moving across open country.

The Marquis was riding very fast, and the horses responded without there being any need to use a whip.

As they went, Narda could hardly believe it was true.

It seemed impossible that anyone could have been so clever.

He had rescued them from what she knew would have been an indescribable hell.

As she rode on, Narda was not really afraid that they would be pursued or prevented from reaching the yacht.

She knew that her prayers had been answered.

God had sent the Marquis to her rescue as she had prayed he would.

On and on they went.

Just as dawn was breaking and the first rays of light appeared in the sky, they came to a lonely oasis.

It was very like the one in which they had camped on the first night.

As the Marquis rode in among the trees, Narda saw there were two fresh horses waiting for them and two men in attendance.

There was also food and drink laid out on the ground.

She was glad to slip out of the saddle.

She ate what was provided and sipped the inevitable mint tea.

As she did so, the Marquis said, and they were the first words he had spoken for a long time:

"As we still have a long way to go, I want you to eat some of this plant which I brought back with me from China. For a thousand years it has given the Chinese strength to endure the longest and most demanding journeys without feeling exhausted."

As he spoke, he handed Narda something which looked like two dried carrots joined together.

"What is it?" she asked.

"It is called Ginseng," the Marquis replied, "and although you will find it rather unpleasant, chew it and it really will help."

"I will do . . . anything you . . . tell me," she answered.

"We must be on our way," the Marquis said abruptly.

He put down his mint tea as he spoke.

As Narda joined him, he helped her into the saddle.

He ordered the two men to give the horses they had been riding something to drink.

He also told them to rest them for as long as possible.

This they promised to do.

Then they were off again.

Certainly the Ginseng seemed to help, Narda thought.

Before they stopped again, the sun was high in the heavens.

It was hard not to complain that she was exhausted when once again two fresh horses were waiting for them.

As they set off, the Marquis said:

"There are still a number of miles for us to go, but there is no need for me to tell you that you are behaving with a courage that I find incredible!"

"After that I . . . would be far too . . . frightened to . . . collapse!" Narda said. "So please . . . give me some . . . more of your Ginseng."

He gave her another piece, and she chewed it as they set off again.

They rode and they rode.

Finally Narda could no longer pretend that she was not feeling as if she might fall from the saddle.

Without her saying so, the Marquis must have been aware of what she was feeling.

He reached out and took hold of her bridle, pulling her horse nearer to his.

This meant that Narda could hold on to the front of her saddle to keep herself from falling to the ground.

"I cannot . . . fail him . . . now!" she told herself.

On and on they went.

At last, when Narda felt she must beg him to stop, if only for a few minutes, the Marquis said:

"The sea is just ahead, and *The Dolphin* will be waiting for us!"

It was late in the afternoon, and the shadows thrown by the few trees growing there were long.

Narda realised that once again they were on the rough, barren ground she had first seen when they left Keniteh.

She looked for the port, but there was no sign of it.

Just ahead she could see the blue of the sea and the land sloping down to what she realised a little later was a sandy bay.

As they drew nearer, two men appeared.

The Marquis went towards them and Narda realised, and it seemed unbelievable, they had done it!

They had escaped from Fez, and now she could see at anchor out to sea there was *The Dolphin*.

The Marquis drew his horse to a standstill.

Then, as he realised she was about to fall, he leapt towards her and caught her in his arms.

She gave a little murmur, and putting her head on his shoulder, she literally fell asleep.

He looked down at her with a smile that was very tender.

Having thanked the two men who had taken possession of the horses, he walked down to the bay below.

The boat from *The Dolphin* was waiting with two seamen in charge.

The Marquis stepped into it, and still holding Narda in his arms, sat in the stern.

She was fast asleep as they were rowed towards the yacht, her eye-lashes dark against her pale cheeks.

He thought no woman could have been more brave.

No woman could have done so much without complaining and without protesting.

It would have been a hard enough ride for a man.

But she was safe, the Marquis thought, and that was all that mattered.

They reached *The Dolphin.*

He carried her, still sleeping, down the companionway to her cabin.

As he did so, he told himself that having saved her, he would never lose her again.

*   *   *

Narda stirred and turned over.

She was aware as she did so that the engines were moving beneath her and somebody had opened her cabin door.

"Are ye awake, Miss?" she heard Yates ask.

She opened her eyes.

"I am . . . here!" she murmured. "I am . . . safe!"

"That's right, Miss!" Yates said, coming farther into the cabin. "But I'd begun t'think ye were 'Mrs. Rip Van Winkle' and wouldn't wake up for 'nother 'undred years!"

Narda smiled.

"How long have I been asleep?"

"Yer've missed one night an' one whole day,"

Yates informed her, "an' if yer 'ungry, His Lordship would like yer to have dinner with him."

Because it all sounded so familiar, Narda laughed.

"Thank His Lordship," she said, "and say I will be delighted to accept his invitation!"

"I 'spect yu'd like a bath first," Yates said in a practical tone. "Yer brought back enough dust with yer to fill a couple of buckets!"

He went as he spoke to collect Narda's towels from a corner of the cabin.

"I'll prepare yer bath," he said. "Do yer want it hot or cold?"

"Anything will suit me," Narda replied. "I feel just as dirty as you think I am!"

Yates laughed.

A little later, as she was lying in the bath, she thought how exciting it was to be back again on *The Dolphin*.

But that was not strictly true.

What she really wanted was to see the Marquis and tell him how wonderful he had been in saving her.

'I love him,' she thought, 'and although he will never love me, the adventure we have had together will be something I shall remember all my life and will tell my children when I have any.'

She went back to her cabin to find that Yates had brought her a glass of champagne.

"His Lordship said it'd give yer an appetite," he said, "an' th' Chef's cooking enough food for a Lord Mayor's Banquet!"

"I hope not," Narda replied, "because he will be disappointed if I cannot eat very much!"

"Yer lookin' a bit 'peaky,' " Yates observed, "an' who'd be surprised if yer do!"

That was true.

At the same time, Narda knew she wanted to look pretty for the Marquis.

She therefore put on the most attractive gown she had with her.

She took a great deal of trouble over her hair.

When she was ready, it was still not dinnertime.

However, Yates came to tell her that the Marquis was in his Study.

The Dolphin was moving on a smooth sea as Narda walked without any difficulty along the passageway to the Marquis's Study.

She opened the door.

As she did so, she saw that he was standing at a bookcase putting one of the books back onto a top shelf.

He turned to see her standing just inside the cabin.

All they could do was look at each other.

Then without saying anything the Marquis held out his arms.

Narda gave a little cry, then was not certain whether she moved or he did, but she was in his arms.

He pulled her close against him and his lips found hers.

He kissed her.

The lightning which had flashed through her body when he touched her cheek seeped through her again.

Now it was more rapturous, more wonderful than anything she had ever felt in her life before.

He kissed her until she felt he was carrying her up among the stars.

They were no longer on earth, but high in the sky.

The moonlight enveloped them in its silver light which also came from within themselves.

Only when the Marquis raised his head did Narda say incoherently:

"I . . . I love you . . . I love . . . you . . . how could . . . you have . . . been so . . . wonderful . . . as to save me . . . when I . . . thought I would have to . . . die?"

"Do you think I could ever lose you?" the Marquis asked.

Then he was kissing her again, kissing her until she felt that no one could know such happiness, such ecstatic sensations, and still be alive.

* * *

It seemed a long time later that Narda found herself sitting on the sofa with the Marquis's arms around her, her head on his shoulder.

"How did you realise so quickly what had happened to me?" she asked.

It did not seem to matter what had happened except that she was now safe with him.

At the same time, she knew she had to fill in the gaps in this extraordinary story.

"I thought it would be morning before you realised that I was no longer in my tent," she murmured.

"It would have been," the Marquis agreed, "if it had not been for a goatherd. He saw what was happening, and as he wanted money, he came and told me you had been kidnapped."

"And you knew it was by the White Slavers?" Narda asked.

"I guessed it from what he said," the Marquis answered. "And that this was the route they took when they came to Fez with the wretched women they brought from England and, I have learnt, from other parts of Europe."

"And will you be able to stop them?"

"With the information that I have given the authorities, and which I am sure your friend Elsie will do, this particular gang will spend most of the rest of their lives in prison."

"I was . . . very . . . very frightened!" Narda admitted.

The Marquis's arms tightened.

"You have to forget what you felt," he said. "This is something that can never happen to you again."

"I could not help thinking how foolish it was to think I could have gone to Fez alone!"

"That is why I took you on *The Dolphin*."

She looked up at him.

"Are you glad you did so?" she asked.

"I can answer that foolish question," he replied, "only by telling you that I love you and that it was Fate that made you appeal to me for help, Fate that enabled me to punish the man who stole your necklace."

Narda gave a little cry of surprise.

"Do you mean . . . the Sheikh?"

"I discovered when I reached Fez," the Marquis explained, "desperate because I had lost you, that the man behind the White Slave Traffic which has been causing a great deal of anxiety is Sheikh Rachid Shriff."

"Will he be arrested?" Narda asked.

"Certainly he will be!" the Marquis replied. "And I left a description of your necklace with the British Consulate, who will do everything in their power to get it back for you."

Narda pressed her cheek against his shoulder.

"Now Ian will not be so angry with me," she whispered.

"No one is ever going to be angry with you again," the Marquis said, "and if they are, as your husband I will deal with them!"

Narda's eyes widened.

He looked down at her with a smile on his lips.

"You can hardly say, after telling me you love me, that you will not marry me! I have already decided that we shall be married in Gibraltar."

"In . . . Gibraltar?" Narda exclaimed.

"I dare not let you out of my sight," he said, "in case any more terrible things happen to you. I thought that while we are here you would like to cruise in the Mediterranean for your honeymoon and perhaps visit Greece and some of the other places about which you have read."

"I can imagine nothing more . . . wonderful," Narda said in a whisper, "than . . . being married to you!"

"I will make it wonderful!" the Marquis promised before he kissed her again.

Although she protested, he sent her to bed directly

after dinner, saying he wanted her to look lovely on her Wedding Day.

As he escorted her to her cabin, she asked:

"Are we really going to be married to-morrow . . . or am I dreaming?"

"I will make you sure of it when my ring is on your finger," the Marquis said, "and no one—no one shall ever take you away from me again!"

The way he spoke told her what a shock it had been when he found she had been kidnapped from her tent.

Although he told her a little of the difficulties that had confronted him when he reached Fez, she knew it was not only that he knew the right people to approach.

His success was largely due to his own determination and cleverness.

He had not only saved her, but the other wretched girls who had been brought from England by the White Slavers.

"I do not want you to think about it anymore," the Marquis said, "but I promise you, my darling, I will do anything in my power to help those who try to crush this cruel and wicked trade."

"When she comes back to England we must thank Elsie," Narda said. "It was she who saved me from being drugged, when, because I was so thirsty, I would have drunk everything that was offered to me."

"We will find her the sort of situation she wants," the Marquis promised, "and perhaps I could appoint her father to one of the Parishes on my estate, where I am sure the Parsons receive a generous stipend."

"Everything you do is wonderful," Narda said, "and I find it hard to believe that I am really going to be your wife!"

The Marquis kissed her, and going from her cabin, shut the door behind him.

As he went to his own, he knew he had found the woman he had always sought in his heart.

Narda would keep him amused and interested and very much in love for the rest of his life.

"She is unique," he told himself as he went to bed.

* * *

The next day they were married very quietly after luncheon in a small Anglican Church in Gibraltar.

The Marquis bought Narda a wedding-ring as they drove there.

As the beautiful words of the Marriage Service joined them for all time, she was sure she heard angels sing, also that her father and mother were near her.

"How could I ever have doubted," she asked herself, "that my prayers would not be heard."

When they went back to *The Dolphin* they were piped aboard.

The Captain offered them his congratulations while the crew cheered them.

There was a wedding-cake which had been hastily baked and iced by the Chef.

When she went into the Master Cabin, which Narda had been told was now hers, it was filled with flowers that Yates had bought in the Town while they were at the Church.

As they put out to sea, the Marquis took Narda into his Study.

"Now at last we have nothing to worry about except ourselves," he said, "and I can begin to tell you, my darling, how much I love you, and it is going to take a very long time!"

"As I love you!" Narda answered. "How could I have imagined when I was so stupid as to go to a party which would have shocked Ian that, because the Sheikh was there, all these extraordinary things would happen!"

"Now you are making me feel as frightened as I was when I rode into Fez!" the Marquis said. "I knew it was only a question of time before you would be sold to the Arabs, who find fair-haired women extremely attractive."

He sighed and went on:

"Fortunately I had good contacts and I think no one would have seen through my disguise except you."

"You know I can read your thoughts," Narda said. "As you came into the room and I heard you speak, I knew you were thinking of me."

"I was thinking of you, and I was more frightened than I have ever been in my whole life that I would not be able to rescue you!"

"But . . . you . . . did!" Narda murmured.

"And now you are mine!" the Marquis said. "I think, my darling, as you have been through so much, we should now rest, not in here, but in the cabin which Yates has decorated for us."

Narda blushed.

"I . . . I would like that," she said, "but . . . suppose . . . you are . . . disappointed? After all, you did not want me aboard *The Dolphin*, and Major Ashley told me very . . . sternly that I was not to be a . . . nuisance."

"You kept out of my sight," the Marquis said, "but not out of my thoughts. I found myself thinking about you from the very first moment I met you. That is why, my precious one, I want to tell you how very close we are in every way."

He smiled at her and went on:

"Not only because we are married and you are mine. We think the same, we feel the same, and we want the same things—and I want you."

He drew her to her feet as he spoke, and they moved from the Study into the Master Cabin.

Because it looked so pretty, Narda thought it was more like a bower than a bedroom.

As the Marquis put his arm round her, she said:

"I am . . . so afraid that I shall do something . . . wrong as I have before . . . and you will be . . . angry with . . . me."

The Marquis laughed tenderly.

In all his long experience with women, he had never had to teach anyone young and innocent about love.

He had asked the White Slavers whether their wares were virgins and untouched, and that was what he had in his wife.

He would teach her about love and make her aware of the glory and the beauty of it, and he would also evoke in her the fiery passions of desire.

It would be one of the most exciting things he had ever done in his whole life.

"I will be very gentle with you, my darling," he said, "but I want you, I want you! Not only with my heart but also my body."

"I love you! I love you!" Narda said. "Please . . . teach me about love . . . and how to love . . . you the way . . . you want . . . me to."

Then as the sun poured through the port-holes and *The Dolphin* moved slowly over the Madonna blue of the Mediterranean, the Marquis made Narda his.

Their love carried them into the sky, they found the Heaven which is the perfection of love that God gives to mankind.

It is what all men seek but must persist, strive, and believe in order to obtain.

Barbara Cartland, the world's most famous romantic novelist, who is also an historian, playwright, lecturer, political speaker and television personality, has now written over 507 books and sold over 500 million copies all over the world.

She has also had many historical works published and has written four autobiographies as well as the biographies of her mother and that of her brother, Ronald Cartland, who was the first Member of Parliament to be killed in the last war. This book has a preface by Sir Winston Churchill and has just been republished with an introduction by Sir Arthur Bryant.

Love at the Helm, a novel written with the help and inspiration of the late Earl Mountbatten of Burma, Great Uncle of His Royal Highness The Prince of Wales, is being sold for the Mountbatten Memorial Trust.

She has broken the world record for the last fourteen years by writing an average of twenty-three books a year. In the *Guinness Book of Records* she is listed as the world's top-selling author.

Miss Cartland in 1978 sang an Album of Love Songs with the Royal Philharmonic Orchestra.

In private life Barbara Cartland, who is a Dame of the Order of St. John of Jerusalem, Chairman of the St. John Council in Hertfordshire and Deputy President of the St. John Ambulance Brigade, has fought for better conditions and salaries for Midwives and Nurses.

She championed the cause for the Elderly in 1956 invoking a Government Enquiry into the "Housing Conditions of Old People."

In 1962 she had the Law of England changed so that Local Authorities had to provide camps for their own Gypsies. This has meant that since then thousands and thousands of Gypsy children have been able to go to School, which they had never been able to do in the past, as their caravans were moved every twenty-four hours by the Police.

There are now fourteen camps in Hertfordshire and Barbara Cartland has her own Romany Gypsy Camp called Barbaraville by the Gypsies.

Her designs "Decorating with Love" are being sold all over the U.S.A. and the National Home Fashions League made her, in 1981, "Woman of Achievement."

She is unique in that she was one and two in the Dalton list of Best Sellers, and one week had four books in the top twenty.

Barbara Cartland's book *Getting Older, Growing Younger* has been published in Great Britain and the U.S.A. and her fifth cookery book, *The Romance of Food*, is now being used by the House of Commons.

In 1984 she received at Kennedy Airport America's Bishop Wright Air Industry Award for her contribution to the development of aviation. In 1931 she and two R.A.F. Officers thought of, and carried, the first aeroplane-towed glider airmail.

During the War she was Chief Lady Welfare Officer in Bedfordshire looking after 20,000 Service men and women. She thought of having a pool of Wedding Dresses at the War Office so a Service Bride could hire a gown for the day.

She bought 1,000 gowns without coupons for the A.T.S., the W.A.A.F's and the W.R.E.N.S. In 1945 Barbara Cartland received the Certificate of Merit from Eastern Command.

In 1964 Barbara Cartland founded the National Association for Health of which she is the President, as a front for all the Health Stores and for any product made as alternative medicine.

This is now a £500,000 turnover a year, with one third going in export.

In January 1988 she received *La Médaille de Vermeil de la Ville de Paris*. This is the highest award to be given in France by the City of Paris for achievement—25 million books sold in France.

In March 1988 Barbara Cartland was asked by the Indian Government to open their Health Resort outside Delhi. This is almost the largest Health Resort in the world.

Barbara Cartland was received with great enthusiasm by her fans, who fêted her at a reception in the City, and she received the gift of an embossed plate from the Government.